Ghost and Tell

THE GHOST DETECTIVE MYSTERIES - BOOK 10

JANE HINCHEY

BAYWOLF PRESS
BP
BAYWOLF PRESS

For Mum—who always asked, 'How many books now?'
Well, Mum... here's #42. 🩶

AUTHOR'S NOTE

Hey! Welcome to the weird and wacky world of my imagination. I hope you enjoy your time here.

If you love anything supernatural as much as I do, then you're going to enjoy the journey ahead - at least I think you will.

Ghost and Tell is the tenth book in my Ghost Detective series, with more to come, so make sure you sign up for my newsletter to get notifications on when the next book is ready.

You can sign up for my newsletter here:
Janehinchey.com/subscribe

Okay, ready to weave some magic and solve some mysteries?

I'll see you on the other side!

xoxo

Jane

A dead teacher. A scandalous secret. And a PI who's way too caffeinated to quit.

Being a private investigator—and a ghost whisperer—means juggling the dead, the murderous, and an espresso addiction I refuse to acknowledge.

When the ghost of schoolteacher Sandra Greaves crashes my morning coffee, she's not here for small talk—she needs me to find her killer. Problem is, her memory is patchy at best, and the only thing she's sure of? Someone wanted her silenced.

The trail leads straight to shady school financials, questionable payouts, and a scandal involving an angry parent and a morally bankrupt school board member. Now I'm knee-deep in hush money, buried secrets, and motives worth killing for.

Meanwhile, my smokin'-hot husband is trying (and failing) to keep me out of trouble, Thor, the talking cat, won't shut up about his diet, and Bandit, my cereal-stealing raccoon, is plotting her next snack heist.

But someone out there thinks I'm getting too close to the truth—and they'll do anything to keep it buried.

Join Audrey Fitzgerald in Ghost and Tell, a paranormal cozy mystery featuring a talking cat, a mischievous raccoon, a ghost with unfinished business, and a murder to solve!

I stood by the counter, my fingers drumming impatiently on the cool granite surface, and locked eyes with the espresso machine. Its sleek, stainless steel exterior gleamed under the kitchen lights, but the machine refused to cooperate. The digital screen blinked an ominous ERROR, and the red light pulsed like a smug little heartbeat. The air was thick with the scent of stale coffee grounds, and the tension in my shoulders climbed higher with every second I remained caffeine deprived. It was one of those mornings when the first sip of caffeine could either rescue my sanity or push me over the edge, and honestly, I wasn't quite sure which way it would go yet.

That's when I saw her. Well, technically, *it*. The dead woman sitting across from my husband, sipping at an imaginary coffee like she wasn't three shades paler than a milk carton.

Once upon a time, seeing a ghost at my kitchen table might've sent me screaming into the backyard. Now? It was just Monday.

"Audrey, you good?" Kade—who infuriatingly didn't require caffeine to function—looked up from his phone. "You're just... staring at that chair."

The dead woman gave me a polite wave and an unsettling smile. "Morning."

Great. Now we were on pleasantries, and for that, I needed caffeine.

"Nothing. Just... zoning out," I muttered, giving the espresso machine a frustrated whack.

Kade frowned and pushed back his chair, calm as always in the face of my impending caffeine-deprived meltdown. "Here, let me fix that before you have an aneurysm."

I should've been grateful, really. Kade could have easily been the guy who didn't notice I was ready to Hulk-smash the espresso machine, but he wasn't. He was the kind of man who noticed. He was also the kind of man who married me three months ago, in a ceremony so perfect that even the ghosts behaved. I was still getting used to being someone's wife—*his* wife—and the way my chest went all gooey when he did things like rescue me from caffeine crises.

Kade methodically opened the lid, removed the water reservoir, and refilled it at the sink. He handled it with the skill of someone who had faced this exact scenario many times before. The machine finally cooperated with a click and a hum, and rich, dark coffee started flowing into my cup.

Without a word, Kade handed it to me, dropping a kiss on top of my head. Steam curled in lazy tendrils, teasing my nostrils with the promise of salvation. I could've wept. Instead, I inhaled deeply, like I'd been drowning and this was my first breath of air.

Meanwhile, the dead woman at the kitchen table studied the entire production, resting her chin on her hand, enthralled. "Is she always this grumpy in the mornings?"

Kade gave the machine a fond pat. "There we go. She's harmless once the caffeine kicks in."

I paused, mid-glare, trying to decide if he'd been talking to me or the machine.

The ghost smirked. "He's cute. Can he hear me?"

"Not a chance," I muttered into my coffee.

Kade glanced over his shoulder. "What was that?"

"Nothing," I said quickly, taking a long, blissful sip. For the first time that morning, I felt my brain flicker back to life.

The ghost snorted, still watching me. "I've been dead for two days, and you're the first person to notice me."

Mid-sip, I froze. Two days? Fantastic.

"Rough week?" I asked dryly.

Kade's brows pulled together as he studied me. "You okay?"

"Perfect," I said, tossing the ghost a pointed glare.

She shrugged. "If it's any consolation, I didn't plan on dying. One minute, I'm grading student papers, the next—poof. Lights out."

"Tragic," I muttered, gripping my cup so hard I was surprised it didn't shatter.

"Mom." A pause. "Mom." Another pause, followed by the soft scrape of tiny claws against the floor. "Mom!"

I turned just in time to see Bandit skittering across the kitchen floor, dragging a half-empty cereal box. She looked up at me, big eyes wide with pride. "Look what I found, Mom!"

The ghost tilted her head, curiosity flickering across her face. "That's... a raccoon."

"Yes," I said with a resigned sigh, glaring at Bandit. "One that doesn't understand boundaries."

"I helped!" Bandit chirped, completely missing the tone.

Kade, who didn't speak raccoon, narrowed his eyes at the chaos Bandit had left in her wake. "Audrey, why does she have the cereal again?"

"She's in a carb phase," I said flatly, trying to ignore the ghost and Bandit's antics simultaneously. Clearly, one of us had forgotten to lock the pantry door, and in all likelihood, it was probably me.

"Mom. Mom. Mom." Bandit scrambled closer, still clutching the cereal box. "There's a lady sitting in my seat. She's weird."

Thor chose this moment to put in an appearance, his gray fur puffed slightly with indignation and his focus locked onto me. He paused at the doorway, glanced at the ghost, then at me, and sat down with a soft, judgmental thud.

"If she's staying," he said, his tone clipped and distinctly British, "she could at least be useful and fill my bowl with kibble. Proper kibble. None of these rations you've been enforcing."

The ghost blinked, staring at Thor. "Who's this?

Isn't he adorable? My, he meows a lot though, doesn't he?"

Thor regarded her with an unimpressed flick of his tail. "I'm just saying it's a thought."

Kade shot me a glance. "Do I even want to know?"

I ignored him and narrowed my eyes at Thor. "She's not feeding you."

Thor yawned dramatically. "Shame. She looks generous."

Kade folded his arms. "Audrey."

"What?" I said, too quickly.

He sighed. "You're acting weird. Weirder than usual."

I turned to Bandit, who was now rolling on her back with the cereal box clutched against her chest like it was a teddy bear. "Bandit, stop licking the Frosted Flakes."

"Mom," she sighed, voice dreamy. "They taste like happiness."

The ghost laughed outright. "Listen to her, chittering away like she's actually talking to you."

Thor snorted and began grooming one paw with exaggerated disinterest. "If you're keeping her, can we at least establish ground rules about breakfast?"

Kade ran a hand over his face, his suspicion

mounting. "Audrey, is it—" He gestured vaguely. "Is there someone here?"

The ghost gave him a cheery wave. "It's me! Hi!"

Kade's phone buzzed on the table, vibrating against the wood. He glanced at the screen, frowning, before answering, "Galloway."

I took another sip of my coffee, watching the ghost while waiting for the caffeine to do its job. She straightened, her brow furrowing as she listened in.

Kade's expression hardened. His relaxed demeanor tightened into something sharp and unreadable. "Where? ... All right. I'll be there in ten." He ended the call, grabbed his keys from the counter, and turned to me. "A body has been found at the Firefly Bay School For Young Scholars."

My coffee tasted like ash, bitter and heavy on my tongue. My stomach twisted, a slow, sinking sensation, as the weight of Kade's words settled over me. "The school?" Firefly Bay School for Young Scholars was the town's only private school—small, selective, and proud of its reputation for academic excellence, whether or not the kids actually lived up to it.

He nodded, slipping into cop mode with squared shoulders. "The janitor discovered her early this morning. It appears to be a murder."

I glanced at the ghost. Her eyes widened.

"Oh, for heaven's sake," she exclaimed, throwing up her hands. "It's me."

Kade couldn't hear her, of course. He turned toward the door, all business. "I'll call you later."

"Wait," I quickly interjected, stepping into his path. "The school? Who's the victim?"

Kade's jaw tightened, his fingers drumming against his keys. "Sandra Greaves. She worked there. Why?"

I didn't answer. My gaze flicked to the ghost, who gave me a small wave.

"Hi. That's me. Sandra Greaves. Teacher, unfortunately deceased, and apparently now your problem."

"Fantastic."

Kade narrowed his eyes. "Audrey. Is she here?"

I nodded. "Yes."

"And? Does she remember what happened?"

I turned to Sandra, raising my eyebrows. "Do you?"

She cocked her head, considering the ceiling for a moment before returning her focus to me. "You know, it's a funny thing, but..."

"You don't remember what happened," I finished for her. "Or how you died." It was a recurring theme with the ghosts who found their way to me after their untimely deaths.

Kade dropped a quick kiss on my cheek. He was well-versed in our grim routine by now. The ghosts would inevitably seek me out, their memories riddled with gaping voids, and it would fall on me to unravel the mystery of their demise. Well, me and Kade. "Call me if you find out anything useful."

The door clicked shut behind him, and I let out a long breath. I turned to Sandra, who was now standing next to Thor, studying him like she was debating whether she should attempt to pat him.

"This is not how I planned my morning," I muttered, cradling my coffee like the lifeline it was.

Sandra crossed her arms, exhaling slowly. "It's not how I planned my week."

Thor gave her an appraising look, his tail flicking lazily across the floor. "If you're staying, I have a very reasonable request involving kibble."

Sandra blinked at him. "Excuse me?"

Thor heaved a dramatic sigh and waddled toward his food bowl, muttering under his breath. "The dead are so inconsiderate these days."

I pinched the bridge of my nose, praying for patience. "Coffee. I need more coffee."

Bandit popped up beside me, cereal still dusting her whiskers. "Mom, I can help. I'm very helpful."

Sandra gave the raccoon a slow once-over, then looked at me. "You live like this?"

"Every. Single. Day."

CHAPTER TWO

s soon as Kade's car was out of sight, I turned to Sandra, who was still focused on Thor. I had a hunch she somehow understood that he had been communicating with her, even though, unlike Dr. Doolittle, she couldn't converse with animals. She hadn't yet realized that I could.

"All right," I said, putting my hands on my hips. "Dead for two days, strangled. Anything else?"

Her eyes widened in shock. "How did you—"

I lifted my coffee cup in a mock toast. "Just a lucky guess." It had absolutely nothing to do with the bruises on her neck. Absolutely nothing.

She stared at me, her expression shifting from shock to wary intrigue. "You're eerily good at this."

"Not my first encounter with a ghost," I muttered, finishing my coffee.

It wasn't that I didn't believe Sandra wanted help—I'd yet to meet a ghost who didn't—but this wasn't a quick-fix situation. No sudden revelations. No obvious suspects showed up on my doorstep with guilty looks and bloodstained hands. And, unlike Kade, I didn't have a shiny badge or access to police reports to speed things up.

I set my mug in the sink, exhaling as I turned toward the hallway. "Let me get dressed. You're coming with me."

Sandra's brow creased. "Where are we going?"

"To figure out why you're haunting my kitchen instead of sipping cocktails in the great beyond."

She crossed her arms. "I'm not haunting anything."

"Tell that to Thor," I shot back, heading for the bedroom.

Throwing on a clean pair of jeans and a sweater, I admired myself in the mirror—until I noticed the stain. And the pulled thread. Frowning, I tugged at the loose strand and, of course, unraveled more of the sweater.

"Genius move," I grumbled, yanking it over my head and tossing it in the corner. Rummaging through my drawer, I pulled out a soft, dusky rose number and gave it a thorough inspection. No stains, no rips, no hidden surprises. Satisfied, I slipped it on and grabbed my boots.

Experience had taught me never to trust Thor, so I inspected them like I was diffusing a bomb. No suspicious wet spots, no mystery odors. Still, I flipped them upside down and gave them a shake—just to be sure. When nothing fell out, I deemed them safe.

Sandra perched on the bed, watching me. "You're really inspecting those shoes."

I sighed, tugging them on. "Thor has a habit of puking in them when he's unhappy. Consider it a passive-aggressive commentary on his diet."

Sandra shuddered. "Your cat is terrifying."

I secured my hair into a messy ponytail as she hovered closer. "You know, considering I'm dead, I probably shouldn't be jealous, but I miss mornings like this."

"You miss utter chaos?"

She gave a small, wistful laugh. "I miss feeling alive." Her voice softened, and for the first time, I caught a flicker of something deeper—loss, regret, the weight of everything she couldn't do anymore.

I paused, my hand lingering on my boot. "You'll

feel better once we figure out what happened to you. I promise."

Sandra offered a weak smile, but the haunted expression in her eyes lingered. "I still don't understand why I found you. I mean, I know I'm dead, but why here? Why you?"

"You're not the first ghost to ask that."

She floated a little closer, curiosity sparking behind her confusion. "So, what's the answer?"

"Short version? I'm a ghost magnet."

Sandra blinked. "That's... not really a thing, is it?"

"It is for me." I waved a hand toward her. "For some reason, ghosts who've died unnaturally—murdered, accidents, take your pick—find me. They're stuck, and I guess I'm like some cosmic flashing sign that says Start Here."

She frowned as she processed that. "And this happens often?"

I grabbed my coat and shrugged. "More often than you'd think."

She studied me, disbelief and faint awe etched across her features. "What are the odds?"

"About a hundred percent at this point." I smiled dryly. "Turns out being a PI and a ghost whisperer go hand in hand."

Sandra hesitated, her lips parting like she had something to add, but then her expression softened. "You've done this before. Solved a murder, I mean."

"Yeah. I have." Ben's face flashed unbidden in my mind—his easy smile, the sound of his laugh, and then that last moment I'd seen him alive. Ben had been my best friend. My brother in everything but blood. The first ghost I'd ever seen.

"My best friend Ben was murdered," I said, my voice quieter. "That's when it started. One day, he was just... there. Sitting on my couch like nothing had happened." I swallowed hard, blinking back the sting behind my eyes. "That's when I knew I could see ghosts. And they could see me."

"And now you help them?" Sandra asked softly.

"Yeah." I shrugged. "Usually, they don't remember how they died. Sometimes they don't want to. But they all have unfinished business. Besides the PI stuff, my job is to help them figure it out so they can cross over."

Sandra was quiet for a moment. Then, with a small nod, she headed toward the door. "I guess I'm your next case, then."

I gave her a faint smile. "Looks like it."

Thor, who'd been observing the exchange with the air of a disapproving landlord, finally stretched, his tail flicking with impatience. "If you're done with your heart-to-heart, perhaps we can discuss breakfast."

"Thor," I groaned. "Read the room."

He flicked his tail, unimpressed. "I did. It's hungry."

Sandra snorted, a small but genuine laugh escaping her. "It's like you're really talking with him."

I lifted Thor into my arms, receiving a disdainful glance as I nestled my face into his fur. "How are you still so heavy?" Despite being on a vet-recommended diet for months, I had a sneaking suspicion that Thor was even heavier than when we began.

"It's my fur," Thor told me, purring as I carried him downstairs. "Fur as lush and dense as mine is bound to add pounds."

"Uh-huh," I said dryly, setting him on the floor at the base of the stairs. "Maybe I need to stop carrying you. A few sprints up and down those stairs wouldn't hurt."

"How dare you?" He sniffed, puffing himself up with mock indignation as he stalked off down the hallway.

Behind me, Sandra hovered, her fingers

worrying at the hem of her cardigan. "What happens now?"

"We dig," I said, leading the way into my office.

Sandra hesitated at the door. "Dig? Like, metaphorically?"

"Yes, Sandra. Metaphorically. I'm a PI, not a gravedigger."

Her face fell. "Sorry. Poor choice of words."

I gave her a sympathetic glance as I dropped into my office chair, which creaked in protest. "Don't worry about it. You're dead. You're allowed."

Sandra gave me a flat stare as I booted up Ben's old computer. It hummed to life with a noisy whir and buzz.

While I waited, I slid a glance at Sandra. "This might take a minute. In the meantime, think back— anything weird happen at the school last week? Anyone acting off?"

Sandra folded her arms, her translucent form flickering slightly as she frowned in thought. "Nothing comes to mind, but..." Her eyes narrowed as she concentrated fiercely. "It's hazy. Like trying to remember a dream."

"Work on it." I tapped the keyboard, muttering under my breath as I typed in the password and pulled up my social media account.

If there was one thing I'd learned in my PI work, it was that small-town news traveled faster than wildfire. All you had to do was check the right social media pages, and today, Firefly Bay was no exception. I scrolled straight to Bay Chatter, the group where breaking news and petty arguments over trash bins coexisted in chaotic harmony.

BREAKING NEWS: BODY FOUND AT FIREFLY BAY SCHOOL FOR YOUNG SCHOLARS

Janitor discovered a woman's body this morning. Police are investigating. The school will remain closed until further notice.

"Here we go," I muttered, clicking on the comments. Sandra leaned in, a coolness brushing over my skin as she read over my shoulder.

Who was it?

The school is a crime scene???

What's happening to this town?!

Sandra Greaves. Saw the name in the news update. Horrible.

I stopped scrolling. "Well, Sandra, looks like the news is out that you're dead."

Sandra's already pale face somehow managed to lose more color, her hand instinctively flying to her bruised throat. "They know?"

"Welcome to the internet." I shot her a glance.

"You said you were at school late Friday night. Any particular reason?"

"Work," she said automatically, but then her gaze flickered away, toward the corner of the room. "I had some... grading to catch up on. And I wanted to talk to someone."

"Who?"

She hesitated. "I don't remember."

I leaned back, the chair creaking in protest. "Okay, so you don't remember who. You don't remember why. But we've got the when. That about sum it up?"

Sandra winced. "It sounds so much worse when you say it out loud."

I snatched my coat from the chair and jerked my head toward the door, signaling her to follow. "We're going to the school."

Sandra floated backward as if I'd threatened her with a cattle prod. "The school? Will the police even let you in?"

"They won't." I smirked, struggling with my coat, one arm in the sleeve, the other flailing around trying to find the hole. "I'm sneaking in. Don't tell Kade."

Sandra looked dubious. "Do you think that's a good idea?"

"I don't have good ideas. I have coffee and a very persistent ghost in my kitchen." I paused at the doorway to look back at her. "Unless you'd rather hang out here and argue with Thor about kibble?"

Her nose wrinkled. "Point taken."

***

The school was cordoned off with bright yellow police tape, fluttering in the crisp morning breeze. Two squad cars were parked near the main entrance, their lights off. Officer Walsh and Jacobs huddled together, speaking in low tones, their radios crackling with static. I stood a good twenty feet back, arms crossed, trying to appear like a curious passerby instead of someone actively planning how to bend the rules.

Sandra hovered beside me, wringing her hands. "This is so weird. I've never been... you know, dead and back at school."

"Well, it's not exactly a class reunion," I muttered, scanning the scene. "And you're not technically here. You're..." I waved a hand vaguely. "Here with me."

"That doesn't make it less weird."

Ignoring her, I continued watching. Officer Noah

Walsh caught my eye, his boyish features creasing with a polite but wary expression. I raised my hand in a half-hearted wave, knowing he'd probably feel obligated to come over and say hi. He returned the gesture and took a step in my direction, but his attention was snagged by Sergeant Addison Young, who exited the building carrying an evidence bag. Addison was all business, her strides purposeful as she barked something at Walsh, who snapped back to attention.

"Okay," I said under my breath, shoving my hands deeper into my pockets. "Time to call in backup."

Sandra frowned. "Backup?"

I closed my eyes. Summoning ghosts wasn't exactly a science, but I'd gotten better at it over time. Most days.

"Ben," I said silently. "I need you."

The air around me shifted, a faint chill threading through the breeze, prickling against my skin. When I opened my eyes, there he was—Ben—standing with his hands tucked casually into his leather jacket, his familiar smirk firmly in place. His presence was as reassuring as the thought of freshly brewed coffee on a frosty morning—utterly intangible yet somehow warming. And despite knowing he was as solid as a politician's promise, I still had to resist the ridiculous urge to give him a hug that would end up with me grasping at nothing but disappointment and air.

"You summoned me?" he quipped, tilting his head toward Sandra. "And look at that. You've got yourself a little entourage."

Sandra gawked at him, her jaw working soundlessly as if trying to form words that wouldn't come. "Who—what—?"

"Ben," I said, cutting her off. "Sandra. Sandra, Ben. Ben's my best friend, former cop, and the original owner of Delaney Investigations."

Sandra narrowed her eyes, confusion mingling with suspicion. "Delaney Investigations. That's your PI business?"

I nodded. "Mine now. But Ben likes to keep his hand in."

Ben gave her a lazy salute, his smirk never faltering. "Nice to meet you. Or, you know, my condolences."

Sandra pointed a shaky finger at him. "Is this what happens when I stick around? You just... summon other ghosts whenever it takes your fancy?"

"Only Ben," I said with a shrug. "Ben, I need you

to get into the school. See what the cops have discovered."

Ben raised an eyebrow. "You want me to do your recon for you? What, can't sneak past the tape yourself?"

"Funny," I shot back dryly. "You're invisible. I'm not. Besides, you know you love it."

"Fine," he said, shaking his head. "But you owe me."

"I'm your unfinished business," I shot back. "Technically, you owe me."

With an exaggerated eye roll, he turned sharply on his heel and sauntered toward the school, a low whistle trailing behind him.

Sandra turned to me, her expression somewhere between awe and disbelief. "Does he always do that?"

"Pretty much." I watched Ben disappear, trying to ignore the weird knot of nerves settling in my stomach. Ben would find something—he always did—but the thought of what lay waiting inside the school made my skin prickle.

CHAPTER THREE

*B*en walked straight through the school's double doors like they weren't even there, his form rippling slightly as he emerged. Sandra and I held our breath as he made his way over to us. Well, I did. Sandra wasn't technically breathing.

"Yep, it's definitely her," he said to me before turning to Sandra, his tone softer. "I'm sorry." He shoved his hands into his jacket pockets, his gaze flicking between us. "You were stuffed into a janitor's closet."

Sandra froze, her face going impossibly pale. "Right."

"The janitor discovered you this morning when he came into work," Ben added.

The silence stretched for a beat, broken only by the distant crackle of radios and the thud of a car door slamming. I glanced at Sandra, her wide eyes glued to Ben as the realization sank in. Not only was she dead, but she'd been murdered.

"A janitor's closet," she whispered, her trembling hands curling into fists. "I—I don't understand. Why?"

"We don't know yet," I said softly, my brain already running through the possibilities. Hiding a body in a closet was a crime of opportunity—quick, unplanned, and done in panic. That didn't rule out premeditation, though. "But we'll figure it out."

Sandra made a face, her bruised throat standing out in sharp contrast to her pale skin. "Who *would* do this? I mean, I wasn't..." She faltered. "I wasn't the kind of person who made enemies."

Yeah, because being strangled and stuffed into a closet screams "no enemies."

"That you know of," Ben said pointedly, though his tone held no accusation. "People don't always show their true colors until it's too late."

I shot Ben a glare. "Helpful."

He shrugged. "Just saying."

Turning back to Sandra, I asked, "Do you remember *anything*? You mentioned being at the school Friday night. You said you were grading papers."

Sandra blinked repeatedly, her eyes narrowing in concentration as she tried to dredge up memories from the murky depths of her mind. "I—I was. I stayed late to catch up." Her gaze darted around as if the details were hiding in plain sight. "And I was supposed to meet someone. I just don't..."

"Don't remember who," I finished for her. "Yeah, we've covered that."

Her lip trembled. "It's like... it's there, just out of reach."

"That's normal," I assured her. "Don't worry, we'll figure this out." I was the ghost detective, after all. "Did you see Kade?" I asked Ben.

"Yeah, he's in there talking to the janitor—guy's pretty shaken up."

"Can't blame him," I said, grimacing. "Finding a body stuffed into a closet isn't exactly a great way to start your workday."

"No kidding," Ben muttered.

I watched Sandra, who hadn't stopped staring at Ben since he'd delivered the news. She looked lost, confused and shaken, her form flickering faintly, as if her emotions were straining whatever tether kept her visible.

"Hey," I said softly. "It'll be fine. We'll find out who killed you, and then you can, you know, move on. Cross over. You won't be stuck here."

She didn't respond, her eyes moving to the school behind me.

"Sandra," I tried again, this time stepping closer. "We'll get answers, I promise. But we need to start somewhere."

Her gaze finally snapped to mine, wide and watery. "Where?"

"Ben, what evidence have the police collected?" I'd seen Addison carrying an evidence bag out to the cruiser, but hadn't been able to make out what was inside.

"A scarf, possibly silk, that may or may not have been the murder weapon. Kade is having it sent to forensics."

Sandra blinked, her hand flying to her throat, fingers gripping the delicate fabric draped around her neck, a deep emerald-green with faint silver threads that caught the light. Her mouth opened, then closed, her expression shifting from confusion to something colder—dread.

Ben tracked the movement, his brow lifting. "Yeah, that scarf."

I exhaled slowly, the weight of that simple

confirmation unsettling. Sandra had been murdered with her own scarf. "What else? Phone? Laptop? Because if they have those things, I'm going to need you to—"

"Do my thing. I know, I know," he cut me off. Ben had the very convenient ability of being able to touch computerized objects and read the data, which negated the whole need to either beg Kade to reveal confidential information or snoop for myself —and despite being a PI, a hacker I was most certainly not. "They were the first things I looked for, and surprisingly—for Kade too—there was no phone and no laptop."

"I don't always take my laptop to work," Sandra said. "And one thing I do remember is that I didn't take it with me on Friday. It's at home."

Pleased that she'd remembered something useful, I smiled. "But you'd have your phone, surely?"

She nodded. "Of course."

I glanced at Ben, who gave me a small shrug. "So, the killer took it," he said.

"Why?" I muttered, my mind already spinning. "Because it had something incriminating on it? Sandra, we need to go to your house."

Sandra looked at me blankly. "I don't have a

house. I have an apartment," she clarified, her voice slightly defensive.

I sighed, exasperated, and crossed my arms. "Apartment then," I corrected, just to please her. "Think about it," I pressed, my voice dropping to a more urgent tone. "If someone managed to kill you at the school, hide your body, and swipe your phone, they were clearly after something specific. Maybe it was some dirt you had on someone, or perhaps it was some crucial evidence..."

"Evidence? Of what?" she interrupted, a fierce frown pulling her brows together. "I'm not like you. I'm not some"—she waved her hand at me—"some investigator, snooping around conducting surveillance on my coworkers."

I opened my mouth to tell her the painfully obvious fact that, despite her protests, despite her denying being involved in anything, someone had wanted her dead. And they'd succeeded.

Instead, I said, "Whoever murdered you snatched your phone. Likely tossed it somewhere, and by now, our odds of getting it back are practically nonexistent. But your laptop is still in the game, and we must secure it, preferably before the authorities swoop in."

Her eyes rounded. "You want to steal evidence?"

I shook my head. "Nope. I want to see what's on your laptop. It could be important. It could help. I'm not going to steal it. I just want to look—plus, Ben can do his thing and sift through the data much faster than I can."

"She's not wrong," Ben added, his tone matter-of-fact. "Whoever did this had to be worried about something—evidence, maybe. Why take your phone? Because they think it had something incriminating on it. But if they discover that whatever they're searching for is not on your phone? Makes sense they'd go looking for your laptop."

Sandra hesitated, uncertainty etched across her face as her fingers intertwined and twisted together anxiously. "But... what if the police are already there?"

"They're not." I turned toward my car, motioning for Sandra to follow. The morning sun cast shadows on the pavement as Ben trailed behind, grumbling under his breath about missing the shopping channel and some new kitchen knives he'd been admiring. Sandra glided beside me, unease practically radiating off her.

"This feels... wrong," she said quietly as I slid into the driver's seat. Ben rode shotgun, leaving the back seat to Sandra. I shot her a glance in the rearview mirror. "So does being murdered, I'd imagine."

Ben snorted, earning a glare from Sandra.

"I'm just saying," I continued, starting the engine, "if there's anything in your apartment that can help us figure out what happened, we need to find it before the police—or whoever killed you —does."

The drive to Sandra's apartment was short, and I spent most of it fending off Sandra's questions.

"Are you sure this is a good idea?" she asked for the third time. "The police will probably be there already."

"They won't," I said for the umpteenth time. "Kade's still at the school, and patrol units will keep the perimeter secured for now. Crime scene processing takes time." I parked a few spaces down from her building, far enough not to look suspicious. "That gives us a small window."

Sandra spread her hands. "A window to what?"

"To snoop," I said, getting out of the car. "Spare key?"

"What?"

"Not all of us have the luxury of ignoring walls," I explained. "Also, I'm going to talk into my phone, so anyone watching will think I'm on a call."

"I'm sorry." Sandra wrung her hands—again. "I don't understand."

Ben took pity on her and slung a comforting arm around her shoulders. "Audrey is the only one who can see and hear us. So, let's just say someone on the street, or even one of your neighbors, saw her talking to us. It'd seem she was having a very animated and one-sided conversation with herself. Therefore, we've worked out a system where she can pretend she's on the phone."

"Oh! That's very smart." Sandra approved.

"I like to think so." I grinned. "Now, spare key? Please tell me you had one stashed somewhere?"

She blinked. "There's one under the planter. Next to the door."

"Perfect." I climbed the short flight of steps to her apartment door, snapping on a pair of latex gloves as I did so, slightly impressed when I got them on with no issues first try. I shot a look over my shoulder at Ben, who miraculously hadn't barged on ahead and instead seemed content to wait for me to open the door the conventional way.

"You're sure you want to do this?" he asked, his tone dry. "Breaking and entering is still technically illegal."

"It's not breaking," I said, crouching down beside

the plant and lifting it high enough to slide my hand underneath. Sure enough, my fingers closed around something cool and metallic. I straightened, holding up the key with a triumphant smile. "See? Totally entering." Sandra hovered nervously at my side, glancing around like she expected the police—or worse, her killer—to appear at any second.

"Do you think it's safe?" she whispered.

I slid the key into the lock, the mechanism clicking softly. "We're about to find out."

Holding my breath, I pushed the door open, bracing myself for the usual combination of awkwardness and guilt that came with snooping through the dead's personal spaces. Sandra's apartment was small and neat—exceptionally neat.

"This how you left it Friday?" I asked, stepping inside. My gaze swept over the perfectly arranged throw pillows, the gleaming coffee table, and the sparkling countertops. Not a single thing out of place. Not even a crumb.

Sandra floated in behind me, her brow furrowing. "No. I mean, I like things tidy, but this is..." she trailed off, scanning the room. "It wasn't this clean. I didn't even do the dishes."

I glanced at the spotless sink. "Damn. That's what I was afraid of."

Ben turned his attention to the door, his form flickering faintly as he moved. "Someone's been here." He crouched, running his ghostly hand along the frame, though it passed through harmlessly. "Careful job, too. No sign of forced entry."

"Great," I muttered, stepping farther inside. "That means they either found the spare key or had their own way in. Would they have put the key back?"

"They would if they didn't want anyone to know they'd been here," Ben replied.

Sandra's hands twisted, her brows drawing together with worry. "Why would someone come here? What were they looking for?"

I shot her a look. We'd been over this already, yet somehow, Sandra wasn't retaining the information—had the way she died impacted her cognitive function in the afterlife? I wouldn't have thought so, and yet...

"They were probably after your laptop," I said. "But goodness knows why they threw in a cleaning service." As I took a step forward, my shin slammed into the unforgiving, perfectly aligned corner of the coffee table. An excruciating jolt of pain shot up my leg, sharp and immediate, a lightning bolt searing through my nerves. The sudden impact left me breathless, eyes watering, as the ache resonated throughout my entire limb.

"Dammit!" I hissed, clutching my shin and hopping.

"Are you okay?" Sandra asked, rushing forward to help, her hand passing through my arm and sending an icy chill through me.

Ben waved away her concern. "She's fine. You'll get used to it. Audrey is the clumsiest person I know."

"I'm fine," I assured her, limping toward a small desk tucked into the corner of the living room and ignoring the throbbing in my shin. "What did you take to work with you on Friday?"

"My work bag," Sandra said immediately, hovering closer to me. "But my laptop... I know I left it here."

I frowned at the desk's empty surface, tugging open the top drawer. "Well, it's not here now. Whoever killed you has your phone and now your laptop."

"Like the classroom," Ben muttered, standing and dusting off his hands out of habit. "They're covering their tracks."

"Yeah, but why?" I said, turning to Sandra. "Did you have anything sensitive? Something that could get someone in trouble? Something they wouldn't want the police to find?"

Sandra shook her head, her expression helpless. "No. I mean, not that I can think of. I'm a teacher, Audrey, not a spy. My life isn't..." She waved a hand vaguely. "It's not interesting."

My skepticism must have been radiating off me in waves. "People don't get murdered over being uninteresting, Sandra."

"Fair point," Ben said, leaning against the wall and crossing his arms. "Something must've triggered this. Think hard. Did you overhear something? Catch someone doing something they shouldn't?"

Sandra's gaze shifted to the floor as she tried to recall. "I—I don't know. I remember being at the school late Friday night. I stayed to grade papers, and..." She closed her eyes, digging for the memory. "And I was supposed to meet someone. But I can't remember who."

Sandra repeated what she'd already told us, with nothing new. I was hoping that with the aid of repetition, another clue may emerge, another memory nudged loose. No such luck.

"Damn," I muttered, scanning the room again. My instincts screamed that we were missing something. "There has to be more here."

I moved to the bedroom, Ben trailing behind. Sandra stayed in the living room, her worried mutterings drifting after us. The bedroom was as pristine as the living room—bed made with military precision, not a speck of dust in sight.

Ben stood beside the bed, his hands on his hips as he surveyed the nightstand. "Nothing out of place."

"Figures." I checked the dresser, rifling through drawers as Sandra hovered nearby, wringing her hands. "Whoever came here was very thorough and very careful."

"That doesn't make sense," Sandra said, her voice breaking. "Why would someone kill me and then come here? What did they think I had?"

"That's what we're trying to figure out," I said, pulling open a sock drawer and finding nothing out of place. "Ben, at the school, what else did the police have in evidence?"

"Aside from the scarf? Just some stuff from her desk—papers. No phone. No laptop."

"Sandra, think about it. Your laptop, your phone—these aren't random things to grab. They either knew you had something they wanted, or they panicked and tried to erase any connection to themselves."

Sandra sank onto the bed—or rather, floated downward until she hovered slightly above it. Her form flickered faintly, and I could see the panic etched into every translucent line of her face. "I don't understand. I wasn't... I didn't do anything."

Ben raised an eyebrow. "Nobody's saying you did. But sometimes people get caught up in things without realizing it."

"Sandra, do you remember anyone acting strange around you? Someone who might've had access to your classroom or your things?"

She shook her head, her voice small. "No. I mean, there were always parents, other teachers, staff... but nothing stands out."

I sighed, straightening up and turning back to the door. "Let's keep looking. Maybe we'll find something they missed."

CHAPTER FOUR

I was back at home, sprawled across the couch with my laptop balanced precariously on my knees, when the front door opened and footsteps headed down the hallway. Kade appeared, carrying two coffees and looking like he'd had a day.

"Tell me those are both for me," I said, sitting up and eyeing the cups with delight.

"One's mine," he said, setting them on the coffee table and shrugging out of his jacket. "But if you're nice to me, I might share."

Blowing him a kiss, I grabbed my cup and inhaled the aroma, feeling my neurons spark back to life. "I thought you had interviews all afternoon?"

"I did. Just finished." He dropped onto the couch

beside me, the cushions dipping under his weight. "Figured I'd check in. How's Sandra doing? She remember anything yet?"

"Not much," I admitted, glancing at Sandra, who was hovering by the huge windows overlooking the backyard and pretending not to listen.

Kade followed my gaze, his expression softening slightly. "Anyway, we got a little more intel. There's talk she had an argument regarding a student last week. Heated enough to get noticed by her coworkers."

I sat up straighter, my investigator brain kicking into gear. "Who was the argument with?"

"Unsure at this stage. We're still trying to piece it together. But word is, it might've involved another teacher."

I glanced at Sandra, who frowned, her form flickering slightly. "Does that ring any bells?" I asked her.

"I—maybe?" Sandra said hesitantly. "There was... something, but it's all fuzzy."

"That's a solid maybe," I translated for Kade. "Her memory's still shot. More so than usual."

Kade sighed, rubbing a hand around the back of his neck. I knew the feeling. Solving crimes would be so much easier if the dearly departed could actually remember who did the dastardly deed. "If she remembers anything, let me know. It could help narrow things down."

"Will do," I said, taking a sip of coffee. "So, uh, have you found her phone and laptop yet?"

"I knew it!" Kade threw back his head and laughed, startling me, so I almost spilled my coffee.

I punched his shoulder. "Don't scare me like that," I whined. "I nearly spilled my coffee. My delicious, very precious, bought with much love by my sexy husband coffee."

"Nice try, but your distraction techniques won't work with me, Fitz," he drawled. "I know you were at Sandra's apartment."

I batted my eyelashes, trying to project an air of innocence. "Who, me?"

"How else would you even know to ask about the laptop?" he said triumphantly, then under his breath, "I *knew* I could smell your perfume."

"Okay, fine, I dropped in to Sandra's apartment. Get this,"—I leaned forward and clutched his forearm—"the intruder, who we assume is the killer, left the place cleaner than when he found it."

"What do you mean?"

"You'd agree that the place was immaculate, yes?" At Kade's nod, I continued in a rush, "Not that

Sandra is a slob by any means, but she says she didn't leave it like that. She left dishes in the sink. And everything was..." I searched for the right word, "... neater than how she'd left it when she went to work that morning."

"That's... odd." He paused, mulling it over. "Not anything I can put in an official report, though."

"Obviously," I snorted.

Kade finished his coffee, placing the cup on the coffee table. "Just... be careful. I know how you get when you're in PI mode."

I set my cup down next to his and gave him my best innocent look. "Who, me?"

His lips twitched. "Don't play coy. You're probably two steps away from breaking into another crime scene."

I gasped theatrically. "That's slander. And for the record, it was one crime scene."

Kade leaned in, kissed me softly, then stood, grabbing his jacket. "Don't do anything reckless, okay?"

"No promises," I muttered as his footsteps faded down the hallway, then the front door closed. With Kade gone, I turned to find Sandra floating by the kitchen counter, almost blending into the shadows. "Well, that was helpful," she said, crossing her arms.

"It was," I said, spinning my laptop back onto my knees. "He confirmed you were ruffling feathers before your death. Now we have to figure out whose feathers."

Sandra frowned. "I didn't mean to cause trouble. I was just..." She hesitated. "Trying to help."

"Help with what?"

Her form flickered slightly, like static on a TV. "It's... hard to remember. Something about a student. There was an incident, but—"

"But it's hazy. Yeah, I've heard this song before."

She gave me a flat look. "It's not my fault I'm dead."

"Fair point," I said, typing notes into my case file. "Let's start with this co-worker. Any ideas?"

"Possibly Priscilla Hawthorne," Sandra said reluctantly. "She's been tense lately. And we didn't always see eye to eye."

I jotted down the name. "Why tense? Personal stuff or work drama?"

"Both, I think. She didn't talk about it much, but she's been acting jumpy for weeks."

"Interesting." I leaned back, tapping my finger against my chin. "We'll pay her a visit. In the meantime, do any parents stand out? Someone who might've been angry with you?"

Sandra sighed. "There was one, during a parent-teacher meeting. He was upset about his son's grades, but I didn't think it was serious."

"And his name?"

She blinked. "I... don't remember."

"Of course not," I muttered, making a note to dig into the school's recent events. If I couldn't get answers from Sandra's fragmented memories, I'd have to find them elsewhere. Letting out a long sigh, I returned my attention to my laptop. "Now, Priscilla Hawthorne. Does she drink coffee or tea? Smoker? What's her social media game like?"

Sandra blinked. "Why does that matter?"

"Because jumpy people like her tend to spill secrets when they think no one's looking. And coffee shop conversations are goldmines."

"You're terrifyingly thorough," Sandra muttered, but there was the faintest hint of admiration in her tone.

"Thank you," I said, fingers flying across the keyboard. "And the parent? Anything you can remember at all? Appearance, vibe, anything?"

Sandra frowned, her form flickering as she strained to think. "He was... tall. Brown hair. Looked like he was ready to pop a blood vessel. Does that help?"

"Better than nothing," I said, adding another suspect to my case file with the note *Tall, brown hair, possible aneurysm candidate.*

Thor sauntered into the room then, his round body looking both majestic and slightly overweight. "If you're planning a stakeout, might I suggest snacks? The kind that fit in a bowl, preferably."

Sandra blinked, brow furrowing. "I don't think I'll ever get used to how you act like his meows are actual conversation."

"My cat talking?" I said, without looking up. "Or should I say, complaining?"

Thor jumped onto the coffee table, his tail flicking lazily. "I'm merely suggesting that you plan this endeavor with sustenance in mind. For everyone's benefit."

My expression didn't budge. "You mean for your benefit."

Thor sniffed, affronted. "What's good for me is good for the household."

Sandra's head swiveled from me to Thor and back again. "It's like you're having a full-blown conversation," she said. "And somehow, you're losing."

"Tell me about it," I muttered, softly closing the

laptop lid. "But don't worry, Thor doesn't come on stakeouts."

"Doesn't mean I don't need snacks!" he complained.

The plan came together with the precision of Bandit raiding the pantry—quick, chaotic, and probably destined to end in a mess. By late afternoon, I had two objectives: track down Priscilla at her usual coffee spot and dig into the school gossip mill for details on *an angry parent.*

"I'm not sure this is going to work," Sandra said, hovering behind me as I slipped on my boots.

"You're welcome to stay here and watch Thor practice his guilt-inducing stare," I said, grabbing my coat. "Otherwise, you're coming with me."

Thor didn't even glance up. "At least she wouldn't try to starve me."

Sandra raised an eyebrow at his plaintive meows. "Point taken. Let's go."

Priscilla's favorite coffee shop was tucked into a corner of Main Street, a quiet spot where the smell of coffee swirled thick enough to leave a film on your tongue. The low hum of voices filled the space, punctuated by the clink of ceramic and the hiss of the espresso machine. Priscilla sat near the window, her body angled just enough to keep the door in her line of sight. Her hands gripped the edge of a folder so tightly that the edges buckled under the pressure. She stared into the untouched cup in front of her, her shoulders stiff and her head dipping slightly, as if folding in on herself might make her less noticeable.

"She's either hiding something or terrified someone's about to walk in and confront her," I murmured, pulling out my phone and opening my notes app.

Sandra hovered nearby, moving soundlessly to stand by Priscilla's table. "She looks... off."

"That's one way to put it." I typed a quick note: *Priscilla—tense, waiting for someone?*

Priscilla tapped her foot under the table, the rhythm breaking only when her gaze darted toward the door. Her phone buzzed, a tiny vibration that made her flinch. She grabbed it quickly, holding it too close to her face, her mouth tightening into a thin line. The screen lit her features enough to catch the flicker of something raw before she shoved the phone back into her bag, stood abruptly, and left her coffee untouched.

"She's on the move," Sandra said, hovering by my side.

I was already up, sliding my phone back into my

pocket, my pulse picking up as I watched Priscilla push through the door. She walked fast, not enough to draw attention, but fast enough that I had to hurry to keep up. She turned down a side street, glancing over her shoulder once before ducking into an alley. I slowed my pace, stepping lightly to the corner and peeking around in time to see Priscilla approaching a big man dressed in dark clothing.

She handed the folder to the man, her hands trembling. The man barely acknowledged her as he flipped it open, scanning the contents with the sharp efficiency of someone who had no time for mistakes—or for Priscilla, apparently.

"He's bad news," Sandra murmured, hovering beside me.

"Glad we're on the same page," I whispered back, my phone angled subtly to snap a quick picture of the exchange.

The man said something, low and sharp, and Priscilla flinched. Whatever was in that folder, it was important enough to scare her senseless. He snapped it shut, gave her a dismissive nod, and turned, his heavy boots crunching against the asphalt as he walked deeper into the alley.

Sandra leaned in closer, her ghostly features lit with curiosity. "Do we follow him?"

I shook my head, already thinking three moves ahead. "Not *we*. You."

Her eyes widened, a flicker of uncertainty in her otherwise calm demeanor. "You want me to—"

"Do some ghost recon, yeah." I tucked my phone back into my pocket. "He won't see you, and you can float through walls. It's kind of your thing."

Sandra glanced toward the alley, then back at me. "What if he's carrying ghost traps or something?"

"Ghost traps aren't a thing." I paused. "Are they?"

"I don't think so, but I'm new to this!"

I waved her off, keeping my voice low. "Just follow him. Peek into the folder if you can. He has no idea you exist, and I'm not about to lose track of him because I'm stuck on the mortal plane."

She sighed, giving me the look of a reluctant participant in a very bad idea. "If I die again, I'm haunting you forever."

"You're already haunting me," I said, shooing her toward the alley. With a flicker and a faint shimmer, Sandra drifted off after the man, leaving me alone in the shadowed alley. The faint crunch of his boots had faded into silence, and I shifted my weight impatiently, hoping ghost recon worked faster than mortal detective work. Sandra reappeared a few minutes later, glowing bright with urgency. "Okay, I've got something. And it's bad."

I straightened. "What did you find?"

"The guy walked a couple of blocks to his car. When he got in, he opened the folder again to check something, and I got a good look inside." She paused, her face flickering between determination and unease.

"Don't leave me hanging, Sandra. Spill."

"Financial records," she said, her voice low. "Payments from the school's budget. Some were normal, but others were... off. Big payouts to Elliot Carter's family, listed under vague descriptions like 'consulting fees' and 'conflict resolution.' But Audrey? I'd seen those records before. I recognized them."

I frowned, the pieces clicking together in my head. "Hush money?"

She nodded. "It has to be. Elliot got expelled after a fight last year, and his parents were furious. They made threats about suing the school, dragging the board through the mud. I overheard it during a meeting. The next thing I knew, everything went quiet. No lawsuit, no more shouting matches."

"And now we know why," I muttered, pulling out my phone to type the details. "The school paid them off to keep their mouths shut. Who approved the payments?"

"Claire Hanover's name was on the documents. She's the one who signed off."

"And you stumbled across this mess," I said, pacing a few steps as the implications sank in.

Sandra nodded, her expression darkening. "I wasn't supposed to see those records. I think that's why... why someone wanted me gone."

I stopped pacing, my jaw tightening. "And now Priscilla has the folder, or had it, and she's handing it off to this guy. What's his connection?"

"I don't know," Sandra admitted. "But whoever he is, he's scary. There's something intimidating about him."

"Agreed," I said, slipping my phone into my pocket. "We've got a school covering its tracks, hush money to angry parents, and a folder of damning evidence changing hands. This is bigger than just your murder."

Sandra floated closer, her features sharp with determination. "What do we do now?"

I met her gaze, a plan already forming in my head. "We follow the money trail. And we figure out exactly how Claire and the Carter family tie into this —and why they needed you out of the picture."

riscilla Hawthorne lived in a neat little bungalow on Maple Street, the kind of place that screamed *I have my life together,* complete with perfectly trimmed hedges and a doormat that said *Welcome.* Sandra hovered beside me as I walked up the path. "Are we really doing this?"

"Yes, we're doing this. She can either talk to me now or after I've rummaged through her trash."

Sandra sighed. "That's comforting."

I knocked on the door, ignoring Sandra, who was doing enough hand wringing you'd think she didn't want me to talk to Priscilla.

The door opened far enough to reveal Priscilla's face, pale and drawn, her eyes darting around nervously. "Yes?"

"Hi, Priscilla, my name's Audrey Fitzgerald. Got a minute?"

Her hand tightened on the doorframe. "Now's not a good time."

I pressed my foot against the threshold, stopping her from shutting me out completely. "I'm an investigator and need to ask about Sandra Greaves. I'm sure you've heard the news?"

Her eyes flickered with something I couldn't quite place—guilt? Fear? Both? She swallowed hard and stepped back, letting the door swing open. The scent of lemon cleaner hit me as soon as I walked inside. Priscilla motioned toward the couch. "You want to sit?"

I shook my head. "No, thanks."

Priscilla crossed her arms over her chest, standing stiffly by the couch. "What do you want?"

I met her gaze, keeping my tone steady. "I heard you had an argument with Sandra before she died. Care to tell me what that was about?" That wasn't exactly the truth, but it wasn't exactly a lie, either. Sandra hadn't remembered who she'd argued with, but Kade had mentioned she'd been seen fighting with someone—possibly another teacher. And Sandra, grasping at fragments of memory, had guessed it could have been Priscilla. Which meant I was throwing this out there and hoping for a reaction.

Priscilla's face flickered, something passing through her expression too fast to catch before she schooled it into indifference. "I don't know what you're talking about."

Sandra crossed her arms, her ghostly form shimmering faintly. "Liar. We argued in the teachers' lounge. Everyone saw."

That was new.

I kept my expression neutral, but inside, my mind reeled. A few minutes ago, Sandra hadn't been able to remember who she'd fought with, and now she was rattling off details with crystal-clear certainty. Why the sudden clarity? And more importantly—why had Priscilla lied?

"Witnesses say you argued with her," I said, watching Priscilla closely. Her face paled even more.

"It wasn't... it wasn't a big deal."

"Funny, because everyone else thought it was."

Priscilla sat down heavily on the couch, her shoulders sagging. "It was about a student."

"Elliot Carter?" I asked.

She flinched. *Bingo.*

"I don't want to talk about this," she whispered,

rubbing her hands together like she could scrub away whatever was on her mind.

"Too bad," I said. "Because Sandra's dead, and that argument might be more important than you realize."

Her gaze darted to the window, fingers twitching nervously. "I really don't know anything that could help you."

Sandra floated closer, shimmering with frustration. "Push her. She knows something."

I took a step closer, keeping my voice calm but firm. "Priscilla, I'm not here to make your life difficult. I just need to understand what happened. Whatever you're hiding, it's better to come out with it now, before things get worse."

Her shoulders trembled for a moment, but she quickly straightened, her expression hardening. "I have nothing to say to you. Now, please leave."

I held her gaze, searching for any cracks in her armor, but she remained resolute. "Fine," I said finally, pulling out my phone and opening the photo I'd taken earlier, holding it up for her to see. It showed Priscilla standing in an alley, handing a folder to a tall man. There was no mistaking her or the suspicious exchange. "But before I go, take a look at this."

Priscilla's face twisted into a scowl, her defensiveness ratcheting up a notch. "That's none of your business."

"It becomes my business when people start dying," I shot back. "So, who is he?"

She crossed her arms, her jaw clenched so tightly I thought she might crack a tooth. "He's... he's a car dealer. I was thinking of buying a car from him."

I raised an eyebrow. "In an alley? With a folder? That's how people shop for cars these days?"

Her eyes flickered with something close to panic, but she quickly masked it with hostility. "Believe what you want. I don't owe you any explanations."

Sandra floated next to me, her expression incredulous. "Oh, come on. She's not even trying to make that lie believable."

I leaned in slightly, keeping my voice low and even. "Priscilla, this doesn't add up. The folder, the alley—it looks shady. And you know it."

She stepped back, her hands shaking slightly. "I said I don't know anything. Now leave."

I held her gaze for a long moment before finally nodding. "Fine. But this isn't over."

I walked out, Sandra trailing behind me. The

door clicked shut the moment I stepped over the threshold.

"That went well," Sandra muttered.

"She's scared," I said, heading back down the path. "The question is, what's scaring her more—me or whoever she's protecting?"

I reached my car, slid into the driver's seat, and exhaled slowly. Priscilla had been defensive, sure, but there'd been something else in her reaction—something sharper. Panic? Guilt? I couldn't tell, but whatever it was, it had her wound up so tight she was practically vibrating.

I pulled away from the curb, thoughts churning. Sandra had accused her of lying. Priscilla had shut down fast—too fast. And the fact that she tried to cover with some half-hearted excuse? That told me whatever she was hiding wasn't just workplace drama.

The realization sat heavy in my chest. A few blocks later, I pulled over beneath the dappled shade of a tall birch tree. I sat there for a moment, staring through the windshield, the pieces of the puzzle shifting in my head. Something wasn't adding up.

Sandra sat in the passenger seat with an expectant look. "What's next?"

Pulling out my phone, I opened my camera roll, zooming in on the picture I'd taken of the guy in the alley. His face wasn't perfectly clear, but it was good enough to work with. Tall, broad shoulders, sharp features—this wasn't someone you'd forget in a hurry.

"This guy," I said, tilting my phone toward Sandra. "We need to figure out who he is."

She leaned in, squinting at the screen. "I already told you—I've never seen him before. I don't know who he is."

That wasn't helpful. And Priscilla wasn't talking. Yet. I didn't buy for one second that he was a car salesman. I stared at the photo, running through my options. I could go to Kade and see if he recognized him, but if I was wrong—if this lead went nowhere —it would be a waste of time. And if I was right? That was a whole other mess I wasn't ready to deal with yet. I loved Kade—married him, even—but I wasn't in the mood for another *talk to me before you do anything reckless* lecture.

I flipped back to the photo. Not handsome. But commanding. The kind of guy who looked like he knew how to take charge—and how to make people disappear. My stomach twisted at the thought.

Sandra tapped her fingers silently against her

thigh, her expression thoughtful. "What if he's connected to the school board?"

"Possible," I murmured. "If Priscilla handed him the folder, he's definitely involved in whatever mess is going on with the school's finances. But who is he? A parent? A lawyer? Some shady fixer hired to clean things up?"

Sandra's form flickered as she drifted through the door and back again. "Want me to poke around? Haunt Claire Hanover?"

I shook my head. "Not yet, but hold that thought."

I pulled up Firefly Bay's local news site and tapped the search bar. If this guy had a public-facing role, he might've been photographed or mentioned in a news article.

The first few searches came up empty. I tried different combinations—"Firefly Bay School For Young Scholars board," "recent lawsuits," "school budget scandal"—but nothing popped up.

Sandra sighed. "This could take a while."

"Yeah." I leaned back, rubbing my temples. "We're missing a piece. Several pieces. And you're sure you've never seen him before? Could be at a fundraiser? Or a parent meeting?"

She sat up straighter. "Parent meeting. That

would make sense if he's tied to one of the students. But I'd remember if he was a parent. Could he be connected to that angry parent I told you about? The one I argued with once. He was furious about his kid's grades. Perhaps this guy's a relative."

I pulled out my notes app and jotted that down. "Okay, that's something, I guess. Let's figure out who that was."

"I don't remember his name. Just his face, and even that's blurry."

Pulling back onto the street, I headed toward home. "The school would have your class attendance list online. We'll start there."

Sandra frowned. "I don't think they post that stuff online. Privacy laws and all."

I snorted. "I have a PI license that gives me access to certain databases. And if I can't find what I'm searching for, I'll send Ben in."

Sandra sat quietly for a few minutes, staring out the window. "So... Ben can really do that? Get into the school system?"

"Ben can do a lot of things. As long as it's electronic, he can pull data from it. Phones, computers, tablets—he even managed to download a recipe from someone's smart fridge once."

Sandra's expression shifted to a mix of awe and mild horror. "That sounds... invasive."

I snorted. "I'm not saying it's ethical. But it's useful. And right now, I need useful."

She shook her head, watching the houses roll by. "Where is he anyway? He disappeared."

"Probably watching the shopping channel."

Sandra blinked. "The shopping channel?"

I couldn't help the grin spreading across my face. "He's obsessed. He figured out there's always someone in town watching it. So, he drops in to watch it with them."

Sandra blinked. "Oh, God."

I couldn't suppress a chuckle. "Don't tell me. You enjoy the shopping channel?" Pulling into my driveway, I killed the engine and slid out of the driver's seat, slamming the door behind me.

As we walked toward the front door, Sandra glanced over. "I have it on for background noise when I'm grading papers at home... do you think?"

"That Ben's ever dropped by to watch TV?" I paused with my keys in hand. "Possibly, but he didn't recognize your place—he would have mentioned it if he'd been there before."

Sandra let out a relieved breath. "Good. That would've been... weird."

Thor met us at the door. "You're late," he announced.

"I'm not," I countered, stepping around him. I'd taken two steps when Bandit came hurtling down the hallway like a furry missile.

"Mom! Mom! Mom!" she chirped, skittering along on all fours before leaping into my arms. Her little paws patted my face with glee.

I laughed, adjusting my grip on her. "Hey, Bandit. Did you miss me?"

Her nose twitched as she sniffed at my jacket, her eyes sparkling with mischief. "Look what I found!" She squirmed out of my arms and landed gracefully on the floor, presenting a crumpled piece of paper clutched in her paws.

I squatted down to take it, curiosity piqued. "What's this?"

Bandit puffed out her chest with pride. "It's a treasure! He dropped it by his car. I rescued it!"

I unfolded the paper, smoothing out the wrinkles. It was a worksheet, smudged with dirt but still legible. Math problems, by the looks of it, with a neatly printed name at the top: *Joshua Craig.*

"What the..." I flipped the paper over. Nothing on the back. "Bandit, where did you get this?"

"From Seb's house," she chirped. "Did you want one? He's got lots!"

I stared at the paper, my brain slowly connecting the dots. Seb was a *schoolteacher.* Seb was my flamboyant, ever-fashionable neighbor and a schoolteacher at Firefly Bay School For Young Scholars. He was also a dear friend—and a convenient connection I hadn't considered until now.

"What's going on?" Sandra asked, her eyes darting from Bandit to me and the piece of paper clutched in my hand.

"This," I said, waving the paper in her face, "is a student's homework that my neighbor, Seb Castle, dropped—and Bandit thoughtfully rescued." I shot a wink at Bandit, who preened at my words.

"Rescued or stole?" Thor said flatly.

"Details," Bandit shot back with a huff.

"Seb is a teacher at Firefly Bay School For Young Scholars—perhaps you know him?" I continued, ignoring my bickering pets.

"Seb Castle is your neighbor?"

I nodded. "Mmm hmm."

"I mean, yeah, I know him, but we're not close or anything. We say hello in the hall, that type of thing."

"Good. Let's go pay him a visit." Swiveling, I headed back out the front door, my entourage of Thor, Bandit, and Sandra hot on my heels as I crossed the lawn and made my way up Seb's front path.

"You think he'll help?" Sandra asked.

I shrugged. "Seb's helped me with weirder things. Plus, he teaches at the same school as you. He probably has access to the school's parent contact list."

Seb's front door was slightly ajar, the scent of fresh coffee wafting out. I knocked gently, pushing it open as I called out, "Seb? You home?"

He appeared a moment later, stepping into the doorway with a grin. His pink linen button-down shirt was paired with dark jeans and loafers, and he looked effortlessly stylish, as always.

"Audrey! What brings you to my doorstep this fine afternoon? Trouble, I assume?" His gaze flicked to Bandit, who was now attempting to climb onto the porch swing. "And what's the little trash panda gotten into this time?"

"She's brought you a present," I said, stepping inside as Bandit chirped excitedly.

"I found a treasure!" Bandit announced,

watching as I handed the crumpled piece of paper to Seb.

"She found this outside your house," I explained. "Recognize it?"

Seb frowned as he smoothed out the wrinkles. "Joshua Craig... One of my students. This looks like his homework. How on earth did Bandit get a hold of it?"

"Dropped it, maybe? Outside your car?" I suggested.

Seb shook his head, amused. "Well, thank you, Bandit; I'm so glad you found it. One less angry parent berating me for losing a student's homework is always a blessing."

"Angry parent," Sandra whispered, her hand going to her throat.

Seb glanced around the room, a faint crease forming between his brows. "Okay, Audrey, who's with you? I can feel a presence. Is it Ben?"

Sandra floated closer, her expression curious. "He can sense me?"

"Sort of," I said, addressing both of them. "Seb can't see or hear you, but he's sensitive to... shifts. He always assumes it's Ben."

Seb crossed his arms, grinning. "Well, if it's not

Ben, then who do we have the pleasure of hosting today?"

"This is Sandra Greaves," I said. "She's the reason I'm here. We're trying to solve her murder."

Seb's smile dropped. "I heard. Hence why I had to cart this stuff home today. School's off limits until the police clear it." He indicated the coffee table overflowing with folders, students' assignments, and homework sliding out.

"You knew Sandra?" I quizzed, taking a seat.

"Knew *of* her, of course. But we were not close, hadn't had the opportunity to strike up a friendship —yet."

"You would have gotten around to it, I'm sure," I said. "So, you'd know about the argument? Between Sandra and Priscilla Hawthorne?"

Seb snorted. "Oh yeah. I heard about it. Sadly, I was not in the staff room when that little showdown rode into town. Just my luck to miss the drama."

"You didn't witness it yourself?" Darn. I'd been hoping for a more reliable witness than Sandra's sketchy memory.

"Nope." He dusted his hands on his pant leg. "So, how can I help?"

I grinned. "You know me too well." I indicated

his laptop, half-buried under papers. "Do you have access to the schoolteacher portal?"

"I do," he said, opening his laptop while I moved to perch on the arm of the couch. "What—or who—am I looking for?"

Sandra hovered over my shoulder, her gaze fixed on the screen. "Can he log in as me?"

"Good idea," I said to Sandra, grinning when Seb raised an eyebrow. "Do you remember your username and password?"

"As amazing as it may seem, I do." She smiled, the first genuine smile I'd seen from her. She rattled off her login details, and I relayed the information to Seb, who began typing. A few moments later, the website loaded, displaying Sandra's profile and schedule.

"We're in!" Seb scrolled through her class lists, his fingers moving deftly across the trackpad. "Oh look, she has Joshua's dad too—Daniel Craig."

"Daniel Craig?" I raised an eyebrow.

"Not that one," Seb said, rolling his eyes. "Different guy. Joshua's dad. But Sandra teaches a different grade. Joshua isn't in her class."

"Ethan. Ethan Craig," Sandra said, looking at me with a strange expression on her face.

"Is he the guy?" I asked her. "Is Ethan's dad,

Daniel Craig—I can't believe I just said that—is he the angry parent?"

"What's this about an angry parent?" Seb asked, swiveling to look at me. "Because I can attest that Daniel Craig has a pretty short fuse. I haven't had too much trouble with him—yet—but he comes with a reputation. He pushes Joshua hard. He expects excellence from his son. I'd assume he'd push Ethan just as hard."

"Hold on a sec, let me get this clear," I began pacing across Seb's living room floor. "Joshua Craig is one of your students, Seb. And his dad is Daniel Craig. Correct?"

Seb nodded. "Correct."

I turned to Sandra. "And Ethan Craig is one of your students, Sandra, correct?"

"Yes." She nodded.

"So, Daniel Craig has two sons. Ethan is the eldest, yes? Since you teach a higher grade than Seb. So, Joshua is the youngest. Right?"

Seb turned back to the laptop and began typing. "You got it," he said, tapping the screen. "Here it is. Samantha and Daniel Craig are the parents of Ethan and Joshua Craig."

"And you're sure Daniel Craig is the angry parent you remember?" I turned to Sandra. It would be nice to be sure before I confronted the man.

"Yes." She nodded empathetically. "Or at least, I think I am."

I tapped my fingers on the arm of the couch, turning back to Seb. "Okay, so we've confirmed the connection. But that still doesn't tell us why Daniel Craig was so angry with Sandra."

Seb leaned back, crossing his arms. "We need more context. If Ethan was in trouble, there should be something in his school records."

I raised an eyebrow. "You can access those?"

He sighed dramatically. "You're really asking me to dig into a student's file?"

"Seb, we're not talking about snooping for fun. This could help solve a murder."

He sighed again, shaking his head. "I know, I know. But if this gets me fired..."

"It won't," I assured him. "Besides, you're one of the most beloved teachers at Firefly Bay School For Young Scholars. Who would dare fire you?"

"That's sweet of you to say," Seb replied, the corners of his mouth twitching into a smile. "Okay, fine. But you owe me coffee. And pastries."

"Deal."

Seb turned back to the laptop. "Let's start with

Ethan Craig," he said, typing quickly. "If Sandra remembered his name, he's got to be important."

The screen loaded, and Seb scrolled through Ethan's profile. I leaned in, scanning the details.

"Hmm... Academic performance has been... shaky," Seb murmured, pointing to a string of barely passing grades. "Not terrible, but definitely struggling."

"Anything disciplinary?" I asked, watching the screen.

Seb clicked on a different tab. "Here we go. He was involved in a fight last year. Looks like it was serious enough to warrant a suspension, but..." He frowned. "It never happened."

"What do you mean?"

"The suspension was overturned." Seb tapped the screen. "Daniel Craig intervened. There's a note from the principal saying it was a 'misunderstanding.'"

I raised an eyebrow. "A misunderstanding that just happened to disappear after Daddy Craig got involved?"

"Looks that way," Seb said, shaking his head. "This kid's got a pattern of just skating by without consequences."

"Thanks to his dad," I muttered. "Anything else?"

Seb scrolled further. "There's a note about Ethan being recommended for counseling, but the parents refused. That's odd."

"Or not," I said. "If Daniel Craig's as controlling as he sounds, he wouldn't want anyone prying into family matters."

Seb leaned back, rubbing his chin thoughtfully. "Okay, we've got academic struggles, a disciplinary issue that got swept under the rug, and refusal to engage with counseling. It paints a picture."

"A picture of a kid under a lot of pressure," I said softly. "And a parent who's willing to bend the rules to keep his kids on top."

Seb nodded. "What's our next move?"

I thought for a moment. "I need to talk to Ethan's classmates. Maybe someone saw or heard something that could give us more context."

Seb tilted his head. "Why don't you come to the school tomorrow at lunchtime? I can introduce you as a counselor, checking in on students after Sandra's death. It wouldn't be unusual."

I grinned. "You're brilliant, you know that?"

"Of course," Seb said with a wink.

CHAPTER SIX

By the time we walked back to the house, the sun was dipping low on the horizon, casting Firefly Bay in hues of gold and pink. Bandit scampered up the porch steps, her tail a fluffy banner, while Thor trotted behind, grumbling under his breath.

"I'm starving," Thor announced dramatically, brushing past me as I unlocked the door. "Do you know how long it's been since my last meal? I'm wasting away here."

"You had breakfast, lunch, and a snack," I pointed out, following him inside. "You're *not* exactly wasting away."

"Details," Thor said, picking up speed as we made our way down the hallway into the open living area—and, most importantly, the kitchen—at the back of the house. "I need sustenance, or I might not make it through the night."

Bandit popped her head around the kitchen island. "What's for dinner? Can I help?"

I dropped my bag on the counter and glanced around the kitchen. Kade would be home soon, and maybe I could surprise him with dinner. I wasn't exactly a gourmet chef, but how hard could it be?

"Okay, guys, let's see what we've got." I opened the fridge, surveying the contents. Leftover pasta, some vegetables, and... aha! Chicken. Chicken stir-fry sounded manageable.

Thor watched me skeptically as I grabbed a knife and cutting board. "You're cooking?"

"Don't sound so shocked," I muttered, chopping the chicken into chunks.

"Should I call the fire department now or wait until something catches fire?"

"Very funny," I said, rolling my eyes. "I'll have you know, I'm perfectly capable of making a simple dinner."

"Famous last words," Thor said, yawning.

Bandit perched on a barstool, her nose twitching as she sniffed the air. "What's cooking?"

"Chicken stir-fry," I said, tossing the meat into the pan with a satisfying sizzle.

Bandit's eyes sparkled with excitement. "Is it for me?"

"Nope. For Kade."

She pouted. "But I helped!"

"Helped with what?"

"Supervising!" Bandit declared proudly.

I chuckled and turned back to the stove. Things were going well—until they weren't. I reached for the soy sauce bottle, only to knock it over with my elbow. Time slowed as the bottle wobbled, tipped, and then plummeted to the floor with a crash. Dark liquid sprayed out in a chaotic arc, splattering the cabinets, my shoes, and the floor.

"Typical," Thor remarked, flicking his tail.

"Not helpful," I grumbled, tearing off strips of paper towel and tossing them onto the puddle. The paper instantly soaked through, leaving me with soggy shreds and zero progress.

Bandit darted around my legs, her little paws splashing through the soy sauce. She lowered her head, her pink tongue flicking out to taste it.

"Bandit, no! There's broken glass. You don't want a splinter in your paw." I scooped her up and set her on the counter, her striped tail twitching with curiosity.

"What's a splinter?" she asked, tilting her head.

I grabbed the dustpan and broom from the pantry, sweeping up the jagged shards. "It's when something tiny, like a piece of wood—or, in this case, glass—gets under your skin. They're painful and hard to get out."

Bandit's nose wrinkled. "Sounds awful."

"It is. And Lord knows I don't need another vet bill," I muttered under my breath, sweeping the glass into the dustpan and dumping it into the trash. Satisfied the worst of the mess was contained, I kneeled on the floor, using a damp towel to wipe away the remaining soy sauce. The kitchen smelled like salt and burned caramel. As I scrubbed, a faint acrid scent tickled my nose. I paused, sniffing the air. Was that... smoke?

A millisecond later, the shrill screeching of the smoke detector pierced the air, jolting me to my feet.

"The chicken!" I yelled, scrambling to the stove. Smoke billowed from the pan, thick and gray, curling toward the ceiling. The once golden-brown chicken chunks were now blackened, hissing angrily in their own charred juices. I grabbed the pan handle and yanked it off the burner, dumping it in the sink before twisting the knob to turn off the heat. The smoke continued to swirl, curling toward the ceiling in dark waves. Grabbing a dish towel, I waved it at the smoke alarm, coughing as I tried to clear the air. The infernal beeping continued, relentless and loud enough to wake the dead.

Thor hopped down from the stool, sauntering over to sit by the back door, his expression as smug as ever. "Told you."

"Not. Helpful," I growled, flapping the towel harder as the smoke alarm wailed on. I didn't hear the front door open, nor the heavy footfalls rushing down the hallway. It wasn't until Kade plucked the dish towel from my hand and yelled into my ear, "Open the doors and windows!" that I realized he was home.

"Dad, Dad, Dad!" Bandit jumped up and down on the counter, her little paws clapping in excitement. "Mom's cooking dinner!"

"Would we call it cooking?" Thor drawled, whiskers twitching.

Pushing open the large glass sliding door, I ushered Thor outside, motioning for Bandit to follow. "Come on, you two, out." Once the smoke began to thin and the alarm finally ceased its screaming, Kade walked over to the pan, peering at the charred remains with an arched brow.

"Was it... chicken?" he asked, poking at the blackened chunks with a wooden spoon.

I winced. "It was supposed to be."

Kade chuckled softly, setting the spoon down and turning to me. "You didn't have to go to all this trouble, you know."

"I wanted to surprise you," I mumbled, suddenly feeling foolish. "I thought it'd be nice to come home to dinner."

He stepped closer, tucking a stray lock of hair behind my ear. His touch was warm, grounding. "It is nice. But you know you don't have to cook for me."

I let out a reluctant laugh, my cheeks heating. "I wanted to do something special."

Kade cupped my face, his thumb brushing over my cheekbone. "You're special. Burned chicken or not."

"Smooth," I teased, leaning into his touch.

"I try." His lips curved into a grin. "Besides, it's the thought that counts, right?"

"Right. And the thought was chicken stir-fry."

Thor's voice drifted in from the porch. "Can we eat now? Or are we just admiring the smoke damage?"

Kade laughed, stepping back. "Let me guess. He's hungry?"

I rolled my eyes. "When is he not?"

"Let's order takeout. How does pizza sound?"

"Sounds perfect," I said, leaning against Kade as he pulled out his phone and placed the order.

The pizza arrived twenty minutes later, and we settled at the dining table with a bottle of red wine. The scent of melted cheese and garlic wafted through the room, mingling with the lingering traces of burned chicken. I poured us each a glass, the wine catching the warm glow of the kitchen lights.

Kade leaned back in his chair, cradling his glass, watching me with a thoughtful expression. "Something interesting happened today."

I took a sip of wine, raising an eyebrow. "Besides Sandra's murder?"

He chuckled, shaking his head. "Yeah, besides that."

I waited, curiosity piqued. "Go on."

He set his glass down and leaned forward, resting his elbows on the table. "I stopped by

Priscilla Hawthorne's house this afternoon to ask a few follow-up questions."

My stomach did a little flip. "Oh?"

"She wasn't exactly thrilled to see me," Kade continued, a smirk playing at the corners of his mouth. "Actually, she seemed a bit... agitated."

"Agitated how?"

Kade tapped the rim of his glass thoughtfully. "She mentioned a pushy private investigator had already been there earlier, asking about Sandra. She wasn't happy about it."

"Pushy?"

"Her words, not mine." He grinned, but then his smile slid away, his face turning serious. "She mentioned pressing charges for harassment."

I almost spit out my mouthful of wine. "What?" I sputtered. "That's ridiculous."

"I talked her down. Wanna tell me what happened? Not like you to go in guns blazing."

I snorted. We both knew that was a lie. It was a hundred percent like me to go in, guns blazing.

"I went to see her for the same reason you did—the argument she had with Sandra. And..." I picked up my phone and scrolled to the photo of the shady guy she'd met up with in the alley, holding it out for Kade to see.

He peered at the screen. "Who's this?"

I shrugged. "That's what I wanted to know. I followed her today. Caught her handing over a folder to this guy—very cloak and dagger. Sandra caught a glimpse of what was inside. Financial records. What looked like payoffs."

Kade sat back. "Payoffs? You sure?"

"Nope." I sighed. "But that's what Sandra said she saw."

"Does she know who this guy is?"

"If she knew, I wouldn't have had to ask Priscilla, now, would I?" I teased with a wink.

"Have you ever thought of joining the force? You'd make a great detective."

"Flattery will get you everywhere." I batted my eyelashes and Kade's eyes glinted. He glanced around the room, his gaze lingering on the corners as though searching for something. "Is anyone here?" he asked softly, leaning in slightly.

"Ghost-wise? No. Ben took off this afternoon, destination unknown. And I think Sandra stayed over at Seb's. Bandit found one of Seb's students' homework, so we dropped it over."

"Good." His lips curved into a slow grin. "Because I was thinking it's been a while since we've had the place to ourselves."

I raised an eyebrow as I stood to clear the table. "And?"

"And," he said, rising from his chair and coming around the table, "I've missed you."

The way he said it—soft, sincere, with a rough edge of longing—had my pulse skipping a beat. I clutched the pizza box in my hands, suddenly hyperaware of how close he was. He stopped in front of me, towering over where I stood, his hands braced on either side of me against the table, effectively trapping me in place.

"What are you doing?" I asked, my voice barely a whisper.

"Making the most of this rare ghost-free evening." His fingers skimmed the edge of my jaw, tilting my chin up. "Unless you object?"

My breath hitched. "Not at all."

The kiss was slow at first, deliberate, his lips moving over mine with practiced ease. The pizza box wobbled precariously in my grip before Kade reached out and gently took it from my hands, setting it on the table behind me. With my hands free, I looped my arms around his neck, pulling him closer. The chair scraped back as I leaned into him, his arm circling my waist to pull me flush against him.

"We've got wine. We've got pizza," I murmured against his mouth, my lips curving into a grin. "This could get messy."

His hand slid up my back, fingers tangling in my hair. "I like messy."

Before I could respond, he guided me toward the window, our movements a blur of tangled limbs and laughter. My back hit the glass with a soft thud, and the cool surface was a stark contrast to the heat between us. His hands roamed, slipping under my shirt, palms skimming over bare skin.

As I shifted, my hip knocked into the edge of the table, sending the pizza box tumbling to the floor. Somewhere between our laughter and gasps, a slice of pizza smeared against the glass, leaving a streak of sauce and cheese.

"Kade!" I gasped, half-laughing, half-moaning as he pressed closer.

"Oops," he said, grinning wickedly. "Guess we'll need to clean that."

"Later," I managed, tugging him down for another kiss. "Much later."

The room was quiet, save for the soft rustle of sheets and the faint creak of the house settling around us. Kade lay beside me, one arm draped lazily across my waist, his breathing steady and warm against my shoulder. His familiar scent—clean, woodsy, comforting—drew me closer, and I tucked myself into him, letting his warmth seep into my skin.

But my mind wasn't quiet. It never was. I traced lazy circles on his forearm, my thoughts drifting back to the case. "Hey," I murmured, breaking the silence.

"Hmm?" Kade's voice was soft, drowsy.

"There's something I didn't mention earlier."

His eyes opened, and he shifted to look at me, propping his head on his hand. "What's that?"

I sighed, turning onto my side to face him. "Sandra remembered an angry parent. She thinks his name is Daniel Craig."

Kade frowned, his brow furrowing as he processed the name. "Daniel Craig? That name sounds familiar."

"Ethan Craig's dad," I clarified. "Sandra had a run-in with him. Apparently, he was furious about Ethan's grades. She thinks it might be important, but she's not sure."

Kade's expression darkened. "I've heard the

name around town. He's known to be... persistent when it comes to his kids."

"Exactly." I sighed again. "It's just another piece of the puzzle, and I don't know if it fits yet."

Kade watched me for a long moment before nodding slowly. "Okay. So, what's your plan?"

I bit my lip, hesitant. "I was thinking... I'll go to the school tomorrow. Talk to Ethan's classmates. See if anyone can shed any light."

His reaction was immediate. He sat up, the sheet pooling around his waist. "Audrey, no. That's a terrible idea."

I blinked, taken aback. "Why?"

"Because talking to kids without their parents' permission could land you in serious trouble. You know that." His tone was firm but not unkind. "You're a PI, not a school counselor. There are boundaries."

I sat up too, wrapping the sheet around myself. "I wouldn't do anything inappropriate. It's just... asking a few questions."

Kade shook his head. "Even if your intentions are good, it won't be seen that way. Parents are protective when it comes to their kids. If someone finds out you've been talking to students without permission, it could blow up in your face."

I sighed, rubbing my temples. "I hadn't thought of it like that."

"Look, I get it. You're trying to help. But you need to be smart about this. Could be there's another way."

"Like what?"

Kade reached out, gently cupping my cheek. "We'll figure it out together. But you're not going to jeopardize your career—or your freedom—by doing something reckless."

I leaned into his touch, closing my eyes for a moment. "Okay. You're right."

"I usually am," he teased, his thumb brushing over my cheekbone.

I smiled, opening my eyes. "Don't push it."

He grinned, leaning in to kiss me softly. "I mean it, Audrey. We'll figure it out. Just... no more going rogue."

"No promises," I whispered against his lips, earning a low chuckle from him.

CHAPTER SEVEN

The smell of freshly brewed coffee pulled me from sleep, and for a moment, I reveled in the cozy warmth of the bed. But the other side was empty, the sheets cool where Kade should've been.

With a groggy sigh, I pushed back the covers and padded downstairs. The sun filtered through the kitchen window, casting golden rays across the countertop. Kade was wiping at the window with a cloth, tackling the streaks of pizza sauce from the night before. He wore a fitted T-shirt that hugged his shoulders in all the right ways, and when he turned, he greeted me with a smile that could melt steel.

"Morning," he said, tossing the cloth onto the

counter before picking up a steaming cup of coffee and holding it out to me.

"Good morning." I took the cup, savoring the first sip. "You're spoiling me."

He leaned in, pressing a kiss to my temple. "Figured I'd start the day on the right foot."

I smiled into my coffee, feeling that familiar flutter in my chest. "You're too good to be true."

He shrugged, a teasing glint in his eye. "I try." As I slid onto one of the kitchen stools, he leaned against the counter. "I've been thinking about your plan to go to the school."

I braced myself. "And?"

"And I don't want you terrorizing kids."

I groaned. "It wasn't going to be like that."

Kade chuckled, crossing his arms over his chest. "Still, I've got a better idea."

I raised an eyebrow, intrigued. "Do tell."

"I want you to come with me. Officially."

I blinked, lowering my coffee. "What?"

"I'll bring you in on the investigation." He straightened, his expression serious but calm. "We'll work together on this."

I stared at him, trying to process what he was saying. "You're joking."

"Not even a little." He motioned to my phone,

sitting on the dining room table where I'd left it the night before. "That guy you took a photo of? He's a genuine lead. And it only makes sense that we pool our resources."

"But—why now?"

Kade gave me a pointed look. "Because you're not going to stop digging. I know you too well. This way, I can keep an eye on you and make sure you're not getting into trouble."

I laughed, shaking my head. "You mean you're tired of me going rogue?"

"That too." He smirked, taking my hand and squeezing it gently. "Besides, I trust your instincts. You're good at what you do, Audrey."

Warmth spread through my chest at his words, and I couldn't help the grin that spread across my face. "You really mean it?"

"Absolutely."

I set my coffee down and wrapped my arms around his neck, pulling him in for a kiss. "Best husband ever."

"Don't forget it."

I was about to tease him more when a familiar chill brushed past me, followed by Ben's voice drifting from the wall near the kitchen. "Am I interrupting? Or should I knock? Oh wait, I can't."

I barely suppressed a grin, glancing at Kade, who was blissfully unaware of Ben's presence. "We've got company."

"Who?" Kade asked, looking around.

"Ben," I said, turning toward the spot where his translucent form hovered. "You're back."

"Of course I'm back." He folded his arms, grinning. "You think I'd miss out on this domestic bliss? Please. Besides, I've got news."

"News?" I arched a brow, intrigued. "Spill."

Before Ben could respond, Sandra appeared next to him, looking frazzled. "Sorry I'm late. I got distracted at Seb's. Do you know he has the cutest mugs? One of them says 'Tea-Rex.'"

I stifled a laugh. "Good to know."

Kade, still oblivious, handed me a piece of toast. "What's he saying?"

"Ben says he has news," I murmured, taking the toast. "And Sandra has joined us."

Ben leaned against the counter, his form flickering faintly. "I poked around last night. Found some interesting emails buried in the school's server. There's a whole conversation thread about hush money and keeping certain things quiet."

My heart skipped a beat. "Did you get names?"

"Not yet," Ben admitted. "But I'm working on it.

They're bogus email addresses. You know the ones. ABC123 at Gmail type stuff."

"How are they on the school server, though?"

"My guess is someone accessed their Gmail account on a school computer, and unbeknownst to them, it saved all that metadata."

I nodded, already feeling the wheels in my brain turning. "That could be anyone."

"Audrey?" Kade prompted, taking my empty cup and rinsing it, leaving it to drain in the sink.

"Ben says there are some suspect emails on the school's server. Not official school email addresses, though, so he can't easily identify who they're from. But he thinks someone accessed their Gmail account using a school computer, and it's saved that data on the server."

Kade's brows shot up. "That's a thing?"

Ben shrugged. "Tell him it's only snippets. And not all your data gets saved—it's the data when you take an action, like print out an email."

"Ah, gotcha." I relayed what Ben had told me to Kade.

"Is that something our techs could find?" Kade asked, staring at the space he thought Ben was standing. I mean, he was off by about two feet, but it was so cute that he tried.

"Doubtful," Ben said. "Not without having a starting point. I could give you the email addresses, though; that may be enough to get them in."

"Here." I held out my phone. "Add them to my contacts." I glanced at Kade. "Ben's giving me the email addresses he found. That way, your guys may be able to find the same data he did."

"Thanks, Ben," Kade acknowledged, then to me, "You ready?"

"Ready?" Sandra asked.

"I'm going with Kade today. To help with the investigation. We're pooling resources."

Sandra frowned. "I thought you were going to the school. Seb said you were going to talk to Ethan's friends."

I cleared my throat, shuffling my feet. "Yeah, about that. Kade pointed out, rightly so, that I shouldn't be talking to kids without their parents' permission."

Sandra stared at me so intently I could almost feel it. Finally, she sniffed and said, "Is that right?"

I was puzzled by her snippy attitude. "You'd know that, though, Sandra. Being a teacher. You know, now that I think about it, I'm surprised Seb even suggested it."

"Well, sometimes you have to bend the rules to

get the job done," Sandra snapped. "A means to an end." And then she disappeared. *Poof. Gone.*

I looked at Ben. "What was that?"

"Temper tantrum?" he guessed with a shrug.

Turning to Kade, I relayed Sandra's odd reaction and her sudden disappearance.

"You think her behavior is out of character?" Kade asked.

"Yes," I said empathetically. "I do. She's been quite meek and mild. Almost timid. Yet just now, when I told her I wasn't going to go and talk to Ethan's schoolmates, she wasn't mad, exactly. More... cold. Like her eyes could cut right through me. But she said that sometimes you have to bend the rules to get the job done. A means to an end. I wonder what she meant by that?"

The unsettling feeling lingered as I grabbed my jacket. Sandra's disappearance replayed in my mind, the way her tone had chilled, her eyes cutting through me like I was the enemy. That wasn't the Sandra I'd come to know.

Kade grabbed his keys and phone from the counter, glancing at me. "You okay?"

"Yeah." I forced a smile, but my thoughts still circled back to Sandra. "Just weirded out by her reaction."

He opened the front door, stepping aside to let me through. "Ghosts probably have mood swings, too. It can't be easy being stuck between worlds."

"Maybe," I murmured, locking the door behind me. "Still, it felt... off."

As we walked to the car, Thor trotted alongside us, his tail held high. "Where are we going? Is it somewhere with food?"

"Stay put, Thor." I nudged him gently toward the porch. "We're going to work."

He sniffed indignantly. "You never take me anywhere fun."

Bandit peeked out from under the porch, cereal crumbs stuck to her whiskers. "Are we going to Seb's again? He has cookies!"

"Not today," I said, shooing them both back toward the house. "Behave while we're gone."

Kade watched the exchange with an amused smile. "It still amazes me that you talk to them like that."

"Who else is going to keep them in line?" I teased, sliding into the passenger seat. Thor, not to be ignored, padded up to the car, pawing at the door. "I still haven't had breakfast. You know, the meal you keep skipping? It's cruel."

"Your kibble is in your bowl, and you know it," I said through the glass, trying to keep a straight face.

"He wants bacon," Bandit supplied helpfully. "He said dry food is beneath him."

"Beneath me?" Thor echoed. "It's an insult to my lineage."

"Stay out of trouble, both of you," I added, waving them off before turning to Kade. "You know," I said, "when I first took over Ben's PI business, I never imagined it would lead to this."

"What? Working alongside your cop husband to solve a murder involving ghosts and talking animals?"

I snorted. "Exactly."

Kade chuckled, his fingers tapping a rhythm on the steering wheel. "Life's unpredictable. But I wouldn't change it."

"Even with the ghosts?"

"Even with the ghosts." He shot me a sideways grin. "Marrying a ghost detective wasn't on my bucket list, but you make it worth it."

My chest tightened, and I reached for his hand, lacing my fingers with his. "You're kind of perfect, you know that?"

"I've heard it once or twice." His grin softened as

his phone buzzed on the console. He glanced at the screen and frowned. "It's the station."

"Go ahead," I said, releasing his hand.

Kade answered, his tone immediately shifting. "Galloway." I watched his expression as he listened, his brows furrowing. "Got it. We're on our way." He ended the call and glanced at me. "Someone came forward. Said they saw Sandra the night she died."

My heart skipped a beat. "A witness?"

"Looks like it."

CHAPTER EIGHT

The drive to the station was quiet, aside from the hum of the engine and the thoughts swirling through my brain. Kade kept one hand on the wheel and the other resting casually on his thigh, but his occasional sideways glances told me he was aware of my restless energy.

A witness. Someone saw Sandra the night she died. My mind raced with questions. Who was it? What did they see? And why were they only coming forward now?

We pulled into the station parking lot, the building looming with its familiar red-brick facade. I'd been here plenty of times—sometimes invited, sometimes not. Today, though, I felt an odd sense of trepidation. Kade parked the car and glanced over at me. "You ready?"

"Born ready," I said. But inside, my nerves were jangling so much they set my teeth on edge. As we entered the station, the scent of stale coffee and toner greeted us. Officers moved through the space, their conversations blending into a low murmur. Familiar faces nodded in greeting, and I nodded back.

Kade led me to a small interview room, where a woman sat waiting. She looked to be in her late forties, with sharp eyes that missed nothing. Her hands clutched a purse on her lap like it was the only thing keeping her grounded.

"Mrs. Parker," Kade greeted, his voice warm and professional. "Thank you for coming in."

She nodded, her gaze flickering to me. "And you are?"

"Audrey Fitzgerald," I said, offering a friendly smile. "Private investigator."

Her eyes widened slightly. "You're a private investigator?"

Kade shot me a quick look, his expression a mixture of amusement and warning, before turning back to Mrs. Parker. "She's here to assist with the case."

Mrs. Parker nodded slowly, her fingers tightening on her purse. "I wasn't sure if I should say anything. But when I heard about Sandra... I couldn't stay quiet."

"What did you see?" Kade prompted gently.

Mrs. Parker took a shaky breath. "I saw her arguing with a man outside the school. It was late, dark. I was walking my dog."

"Do you know what time this was?" I asked.

She thought for a moment. "Around ten, maybe a little later. I remember checking my watch because I was debating if it was too late to be out."

"Do you know who the man was?" I pressed.

She shook her head. "No. But he was tall, broad-shouldered. He seemed... angry."

My pulse quickened. "Did you hear what they were arguing about?"

Mrs. Parker hesitated before shaking her head again. "No, I—I didn't hear anything clearly. Only their voices. The way they were speaking—it was tense. Heated."

Kade and I exchanged a look. That lined up with what we knew—Sandra had caught someone sneaking around the school and run him off.

"Anything else?" Kade asked.

Mrs. Parker's brows pulled together. "I saw them

go around the side of the building. I thought it was odd, but I didn't think too much of it at the time. Then, when I heard Sandra was dead…"

"You did the right thing by coming forward," Kade assured her.

She nodded, though she still looked uneasy. "I hope it helps."

"It does," I said firmly. "More than you know."

As Mrs. Parker left, Kade turned to me. "What are you thinking?"

"I'm thinking this isn't just about a school scandal." I tapped my fingers on the table. "It's about covering up something bigger. Something worth killing for."

Kade's jaw tightened. "And we're getting closer to finding out what." Then his phone buzzed. He glanced at the screen, his expression darkening.

"What is it?" I asked.

"Priscilla Hawthorne." He stood, grabbing his jacket. "She just called the station. Said someone broke into her house."

My blood ran cold. "Think it's connected?"

"I'd bet my badge on it."

By the time we pulled up outside Priscilla's house, my nerves were buzzing like Thor after discovering an unattended roast chicken. The house, which yesterday had screamed *suburban perfection*, still looked pristine from the outside—but now it felt off. Like the illusion had cracked, even if you couldn't see it from the curb.

Kade turned off the engine and gave me a quick glance. "You good?"

I rolled my shoulders, trying to shake the tension. "Define good."

He smirked faintly. "Not about to charge in and yell at Priscilla again?"

I shot him a look. "You make it sound like I do that regularly."

"You do that *regularly*," he said, pushing open the door before I could respond.

"Not every time," I muttered, stepping out of the car and immediately stumbling on the curb. Because, *of course, I did*. Kade didn't comment, though the corner of his mouth twitched. Instead, he gestured toward Priscilla, who was perched on the porch steps. Her arms were wrapped so tightly around herself, I half-expected her to implode. Her eyes flicked between Kade and me, landing on me last, where they narrowed into slits.

"Ms. Hawthorne," Kade called, his cop voice dialed up to soothing-but-firm. He approached her with deliberate steps, the embodied equivalent of *I'm here to help, not arrest you.* "Are you all right?"

She shook her head, her voice barely above a whisper. "I—I was out this morning, running errands. When I got back, the door was open. And everything inside..." Her voice wavered, and she pressed her lips together like she was trying to keep the words—or maybe a sob—from escaping.

"You didn't see anyone?" Kade asked gently.

"No," she whispered, then glanced at me with a glare sharp enough to cut steel. "What's she doing here? She's not the police."

Before I could respond, Kade stepped in, his tone soft but firm. "Audrey's assisting with the investigation. She's a private investigator working with me."

Priscilla's lips thinned. "I don't want her... interfering."

"Noted," Kade replied, clearly unfazed. "Why don't you wait out here? We'll take a look inside and let you know what we find."

Priscilla nodded stiffly, perching on the edge of the top step like she might bolt at the first sign of danger. Her knuckles were white from gripping her arms so tightly, and for a second, I almost felt sorry for her. *Almost.*

Kade pulled on a pair of gloves from his jacket pocket and glanced at me. "Ready?"

I mirrored his action, tugging on my own gloves. "Yep."

The first thing that hit me when we stepped inside was the smell—something sharp and acrid mixed with an underlying sourness that had my nose wrinkling in protest. Priscilla's house had smelled like lemon cleaner when I visited yesterday. Now it smelled like something had been torched.

"Lovely," I muttered, stepping over an overturned vase that had given its life for the cause. The living room was chaos. Cushions were slashed, drawers yanked out and emptied, and papers scattered like confetti after a parade. Someone had been on a mission.

Kade crouched near the coffee table, inspecting something I couldn't see from my angle. "This wasn't random."

"You don't think so?" I said, stepping over a toppled chair. My boot crunched on something, and I winced, lifting my foot to reveal the remains of a porcelain cat figurine. "RIP, Kitty."

Kade glanced up, his lips twitching. "Focus, Audrey."

"I am focused," I protested. "Do you think

whoever did this was looking for something specific? Or did they just want to vandalize the place?"

"The former. The mess is to hide that they were looking for something specific." Kade stood, his gaze scanning the room. "But what?"

I moved toward the kitchen, the acrid stench stronger here, and stopped short. A couch cushion—scorched, half-melted—sat in the sink, its stuffing spilling out. I gestured toward it. "Well, that explains the smell."

Kade stepped closer, inspecting the charred edges. "They weren't trying to burn the place down."

"Nope," I agreed. "They wanted to send a message. If they wanted a fire, they would've torched the entire sofa, not a cushion in the sink."

Kade exhaled slowly. "They wanted to rattle her."

"Looks like it worked," I muttered, glancing back at the wreckage.

I crouched near an overturned sideboard, brushing aside the debris until my fingers landed on something solid. A piece of torn cream-colored paper, thicker than the others, caught my eye. The printed words were faint but legible: *...approval for funds... confidential... finalize by next quarter.*

I held it up for Kade. "This might be something."

He took it, reading the visible text, his expression hardening. "This ties to the school."

"Definitely," I agreed, glancing at the surrounding chaos. "Priscilla handed over that folder yesterday, but maybe she didn't give him everything."

"Insurance," Kade muttered, slipping the paper into an evidence bag. "If she kept copies, it's not hard to imagine why someone would come after her."

"Or why Sandra ended up dead," I said, the words heavy. "Two teachers from the same school? It can't be a coincidence."

Kade's gaze flicked to me, his expression unreadable. "And the guy in the alley? If he's connected to this, he's not just some random middleman."

I nodded, my mind spinning. "The financial reports Priscilla handed over could be the key. What if the break-in wasn't about what Priscilla kept, but who might still know about it? If Sandra stumbled across the same records..."

"She'd be a loose end," Kade finished grimly. "And if someone's cleaning up, Priscilla's lucky to still be breathing."

I shivered, glancing toward the doorway where

Priscilla waited on the porch steps. "What do we tell her?"

"That we'll keep looking," Kade said, his voice steady. "And that she needs to be careful."

I sighed, rubbing the back of my neck. "This still doesn't answer the big question. What's in those financial records that's worth killing for?"

"Money," Kade said simply. "It's always about money."

"But whose money?" I pressed. "And where's it going?"

"That's the million-dollar question." His gaze gave one last sweep of the ransacked room. "Let's wrap up here. I'll call in a forensics team, and in the meantime, we'll take Priscilla to the station—get a timeline, and see if she noticed anything before she left this morning."

"And ask her about the guy in the alley. And the folder," I added. "She didn't want to tell me, but I have a feeling after this"—I gestured at the surrounding wreckage—"she might be more willing to talk. Especially once she realizes I already shared the photo with the police."

Kade's lips curled. "Thanks, my little ghost detective; how would I ever do my job without you?"

CHAPTER NINE

The interrogation room at the station wasn't designed for comfort—or maybe it was, if your idea of comfort involved stark lighting and chairs that made your butt feel like you'd been sitting on concrete for three days straight. I perched on the edge of my seat, trying to look professional and not like I was silently worrying about developing hemorrhoids.

Across from me, Priscilla Hawthorne sat stiffly, her lips pulled into a taut line, arms crossed in a way that screamed *defensive*. Her perfume—a sharp floral —hung in the air, mingling with the faint scent of stale coffee from the nearby break room. I offered her a cup to ease the tension, but she waved it off like I'd suggested arsenic.

Kade, ever the steady hand, started things off. "Thanks for coming in, Ms. Hawthorne."

Priscilla's gaze flicked to him, then to me, narrowing just a touch. "Do I have a choice?" she asked, her tone clipped.

I leaned back, plastering on my best disarming smile. "You do, actually. But you chose to show up, which makes you smarter than most people."

She didn't look impressed. If anything, her glare deepened, and for a second, I thought she might actually sprout claws.

Kade cleared his throat, pulling her attention back to him. "We're trying to get a clearer picture of what happened at your house."

Priscilla's laugh was sharp and humorless. "You mean the break-in? You'd think I was the one who smashed up the place, the way you're treating me."

"I can see how it might feel that way," Kade said, his tone level. "But if we're going to find out who's behind this, we need your help."

Sandra's ghost materialized out of nowhere, striding straight through me before I could even register her presence. An arctic chill engulfed me, sharp and unforgiving, instantly freezing the breath in my lungs. I gasped, instinctively recoiling, my coffee teetering precariously close to the table's edge as I gripped my chair for support.

Kade glanced at me, his brow furrowing. "You okay?"

"Fine," I said quickly, waving him off as I forced a smile. My heart raced as the lingering frost of Sandra's ghostly walk-through settled into my bones. "Cold all of a sudden."

Sandra, completely unfazed by her unintentional assault, planted herself near the corner of the room, arms crossed, her expression as unimpressed as Priscilla's. "She's lying already," Sandra said, shaking her head with an exasperated sigh. "She knows exactly why someone broke into her house."

I fought the urge to respond directly, swallowing hard and forcing my attention back to Priscilla. Sandra's voice was sharp and clear, but Kade, blissfully unaware of the commentary, kept his gaze firmly on our reluctant witness.

Ben popped in behind her, leaning casually against the wall. "This is going to be good," he said, grinning. "I bet she folds in under ten minutes."

"Quiet," I muttered under my breath.

Priscilla's brows shot up. "Excuse me?"

Crap. "I said, quite a mess, huh? Your house."

Kade gave me a sidelong glance that screamed, *get it together!* I cleared my throat, sitting up straighter.

"So," Kade continued smoothly, "you mentioned nothing seemed stolen. Is there anything you can think of that someone might've been looking for?"

Priscilla hesitated, her fingers twitching against the strap of her purse. "No," she said finally, though the word came out a little too fast, a little too sharp.

Sandra leaned closer to me, her ghostly presence sending a chill down my spine. "Push her," she urged. "Ask her about the folder."

I kept my focus on Priscilla, trying to ignore the ghosts hovering nearby. "Are you sure?" I asked, tilting my head. "Because this didn't look like a smash-and-grab. It looked like someone was looking for something."

Her gaze darted to the side, her lips tightening. "I don't know what you mean."

Ben snorted. "Oh, come on! You're about as convincing as a raccoon caught in a garbage bin."

Kade leaned forward, his tone soft but firm. "Priscilla, if you're withholding something, now's the time to come clean. We're not here to judge—"

"Speak for yourself," Sandra muttered.

"—we just want to understand why you were targeted."

"Perhaps I can help," I said, pulling up the photo of the dodgy guy in the alley on my phone. The one where Priscilla was handing him a folder. "Is there any chance it was related to this?"

Priscilla's shoulders tensed, and for a moment, I thought she might bolt. "I told you. I'm thinking of buying a car." It sounded weak, even to my ears.

"Liar, liar, pants on fire," Sandra chanted.

"What was in the folder?" I pressed.

Ben folded his arms, watching Priscilla carefully. "She's cornered," he murmured. "Press harder, but don't spook her. She wants to talk—she just doesn't know how much trouble she's in yet."

Oh, how I wished the dearly departed would shut up. It was taking everything I had to maintain my focus on Priscilla and not on the infernal chatter from Ben and Sandra.

"She's not going to cave," Sandra pouted, crossing her arms and drifting back and forth behind Priscilla's chair.

"Yeah, she will. This is a woman with a lot on her conscience. She'll spill."

Priscilla sighed, her fingers twisting the strap of

her purse until it looked ready to snap. "Fine," she said, her voice low. "They were... documents."

Kade's eyes sharpened. "What kind of documents?"

She hesitated again, the battle playing out on her face. Finally, she blurted, "Financial records. From the school."

I exchanged a glance with Kade, my pulse quickening. "You took financial records from the school?"

She nodded reluctantly. "I found them in Claire Hanover's office. They... didn't look right."

Ben whistled low. "Bingo."

Sandra narrowed her eyes at Priscilla. "That's not the whole story. What was she doing in Claire's office? That's theft."

"Why didn't you go to the authorities?" Kade asked, his voice calm but probing.

Priscilla's jaw clenched, her gaze dropping to the table. "Because... because I wasn't supposed to be in her office. And because..." She trailed off, her face flushing. "I've told you everything I know. Why would someone break into my home? I don't have anything. I'm the victim here!"

"Ask her about her little 'meetings' with Daniel Craig. She's been cozying up to him for months,"

Sandra muttered, clearly unimpressed with her co-worker.

"Daniel Craig?" I repeated, not realizing I'd spoken aloud until Priscilla stiffened in her seat, her eyes darting to me.

"What about him?"

"Oh, um, I was wondering if you had either of his sons in your class?" I floundered.

She frowned. "What on earth does that have to do with anything?"

I shrugged. "Just curious."

Kade gave me the side-eye. And who could blame him? I'd gone off on a tangent that only made sense to the ghosts in the room.

"I'm not sure what Daniel Craig has to do with this," Priscilla said, her voice clipped.

Kade, perceptive as ever, leaned forward. "It's a fair question, Ms. Hawthorne. You've been at the school long enough to notice patterns. Has Mr. Craig ever been involved in school matters that seemed... unusual?"

Priscilla hesitated, her mouth opening and closing, but no words coming out. Finally, she huffed. "He's a parent. A wealthy, influential parent. Of course, he's involved."

"Involved how?" I pressed, ignoring the curious

tilt of Kade's head as I leaned forward, resting my chin on my hands in a way that would look casual if I weren't holding my breath.

Her lips pressed into a thin line, and for a moment, I thought she wouldn't answer. Then, almost reluctantly, she said, "He's donated a lot of money to the school over the years. For upgrades, programs. The kind of donations that keep the lights on."

"And grease the wheels?" Kade asked, his tone steady, his eyes sharp.

Priscilla flushed, but she didn't deny it. "Look, I don't know what you're trying to imply, but I haven't done anything wrong."

Sandra let out a derisive laugh, circling the room. "Oh, sure. She's as innocent as a shark at a seal convention."

"Why don't you let us decide that?" Kade said. "We're trying to help you, Ms. Hawthorne, but you need to give us something to work with. If you don't, you're just making yourself look guilty."

Her head snapped up, eyes blazing. "Guilty of what? Someone broke into my house! Why am I the one on trial here?"

"Because you're not telling the whole truth," I said, leaning in. "And we both know it."

Priscilla's jaw clenched, and for a moment, the room was so silent I could hear my heartbeat thudding in my ears. Then, just as I thought she'd clam up completely, she muttered, "Fine."

Kade and I exchanged a glance, and Sandra gave an encouraging nod from the corner.

"I found something," Priscilla said, her voice low. "In Claire Hanover's office."

"What kind of something?" Kade asked.

She hesitated again. "The financial records I took—they pointed to payouts. Large ones. To a family."

"The Carters?" I asked, my pulse quickening.

Priscilla's head snapped toward me, her eyes narrowing. "How do you know about the Carters?"

Sandra hovered by my shoulder, her voice icy. "Tell her you saw the folder. She'll believe that."

I shot her a subtle look, resisting the urge to snap, "Thanks for nothing, ghost." Instead, I kept my tone measured. "You're not the only one who's noticed something off, Priscilla. The name's come up before."

Her gaze darted between Kade and me. "The records didn't say why they were paid. Just that it was a significant amount of money."

"And you didn't report it?" Kade asked, his tone pointed.

Priscilla scoffed. "To who? Claire's Vice Principal of the school. Untouchable. And I wasn't about to risk my job over something I couldn't even prove was illegal."

"Yet you took the documents and gave them to someone," I said, indicating the photo on my phone again. "Who's this guy, Priscilla?"

Priscilla hesitated, her panic palpable. "I don't know. I swear. He said he'd take care of it. That it would... keep me out of trouble."

I exchanged a glance with Kade, my stomach twisting. "And you believed him?"

"I didn't know what else to do," she whispered. "I thought I was protecting myself."

Kade's voice was low, almost a growl. "And now you're in the middle of something far bigger than you realized."

The room fell silent, the weight of her choices hanging heavy in the air. I glanced at Sandra, who was watching Priscilla with an expression I couldn't quite place. Sympathy? Disappointment? It was hard to tell with ghosts.

"Well," Ben drawled from his corner. "This just got interesting."

I stared at Priscilla, struggling to wrap my head around it. "You really thought handing over confidential documents to some random guy would keep you safe?" My voice came out sharper than I intended, but seriously—what was she thinking? "That's not self-preservation. It's a death wish."

"Look, I panicked!" she snapped, her defensiveness flaring again. "I didn't know what to do. And then Sandra ended up dead, and I—" Her breath hitched, her palms pressing hard against her cheeks. "I thought if I handed over the documents, maybe it would all just... go away. Like I could make it someone else's problem."

Kade interjected, his voice steady. "You need to tell us everything you know. If you want to help yourself, you can't leave anything out."

Priscilla nodded, a hint of determination flickering in her eyes. "Okay. I saw the financial records, but I didn't understand all of it. I just knew it was bad. So, I took them." She gestured helplessly. "I thought it was a good idea at the time. Then I got the threats. I had no idea it would lead to this."

That caught my attention. "What threats?"

"A threatening phone call. It was one of those digitized voices. You know, the ones that make your voice sound funny so you can't be identified?"

"What did they say?" Kade asked.

Priscilla chewed her lip. "Um. Just that they

knew I'd taken the folder from Claire's office, and if I didn't want anything bad to happen, then I was to meet the man in the alley and hand it over."

"Bad to happen? Did they threaten you physically?" I was aghast. How awful.

But Priscilla shook her head. "Worse," she whispered. "They had certain, er"—she cleared her throat—"photos..." She paused, her cheeks flushing before saying in a rush, "They threatened to go public with them, not only send them to the school board but post them on social media and the Firefly Bay Tribune."

Kade and I exchanged a look. *Nudes.* It had to be.

"Who took the photos? Who else knew about them?" Kade asked.

She took a deep breath, her gaze dropping as she struggled with the weight of it all. "Someone I thought I could trust. It doesn't matter..." Her voice trailed off, a shadow of doubt creeping into her features.

Kade leaned forward, his eyes narrowing. "Who was it?"

Priscilla remained silent for a moment, mulling over her choices. I knew the second she squared her shoulders and lifted her chin that she'd made a decision, and it was not going to swing in our favor.

"I've said all I'm prepared to say on that matter," she declared. "It's not relevant to my break-in." Clasping her purse, she surged to her feet, almost knocking her chair over.

"Before you go—" I reached out as if to grab her wrist but stopped short of touching her. "One last quick question. I promise it's not about the photos."

She sniffed. "Fine. What?"

"Why did you go into Claire's office in the first place?" It had been niggling in the back of my mind. Did Priscilla go into Claire's office to snoop? And if so, why? What was she looking for? Did she have an inkling about the shenanigans around the school's finances? Or was it something else altogether?

Her answer was quick, fast, and rehearsed. "I was dropping off the absenteeism report she requested at the last staff meeting." She shrugged. "She wasn't in her office, so I left it in her in-tray."

"So, you were snooping," I said bluntly, ignoring Kade's sidelong glance. "And you found the financial records by accident?"

Priscilla's jaw worked as she struggled for a response. "It wasn't like I planned to steal them. But when I saw what they were... it didn't look right. I thought maybe they were evidence of something."

"Evidence of what?" Kade pressed, leaning forward.

"I don't know," Priscilla snapped, her voice cracking. "But it wasn't normal. Payouts that large to a single family? It raised red flags."

"And you decided the best course of action was to take them and give them to someone you couldn't even identify," Kade said, his voice hardening. "Does that sound normal to you?"

Priscilla flinched at his tone, her shoulders hunching. "I thought it would protect me. That he—whoever he was—would make it go away. I didn't want to be dragged into anything illegal."

"Why were you so worried about being dragged into it?" I asked, narrowing my eyes. "Finding the documents wasn't illegal, was it?"

Priscilla shrugged, sliding her purse strap over her shoulder. "Now, if you'll excuse me, I have a mess to sort out at home."

Kade stood and opened the door for her, watching Priscilla make her way down the passageway before turning to look at me, one brow raised.

"She's lying through her teeth," we said in unison.

CHAPTER TEN

Kade's hands rested lightly on the steering wheel, his attention flicking between the road and me. The station loomed behind us, but I couldn't shake the prickly unease that had followed me out of the interrogation room. Priscilla Hawthorne had played her cards close to her chest, but something about her story didn't sit right. A missing piece. A lie tucked between the truths. I just had to pry it loose.

"You're awfully quiet," Kade said. His tone was light, but his gaze flicked toward me, assessing. "Or is it just weirdly peaceful without the peanut gallery chiming in?"

I blinked, then realized what he meant. Ben and Sandra. They'd been running their mouths non-stop during the interview, but now the car was blissfully —eerily—silent.

"They're not here," I admitted.

His brows lifted slightly. "That a first?"

I huffed out a breath. "Not quite. Sometimes they disappear for a bit, but they always come back. Eventually."

Kade was quiet for a beat, processing that. Then, "Any idea where they went?"

I stared out the window, rolling the thought over. "Sandra was practically vibrating with frustration over Priscilla. If I had to guess, she's following her. And Ben…" I sighed. "Ben could be doing anything, but the shopping channel is always a strong possibility."

Kade made a considering noise, turning onto my street. "So, you're telling me I could've had a ghost-free drive this whole time? That this level of peace and quiet was an option?"

I shot him a look. "Don't get used to it."

His lips twitched, but he kept his eyes on the road. "I wouldn't dare."

The streets blurred past as the car hummed along, the faint tang of coffee still clinging to my senses from the station. The quiet stretched out, and my mind circled back to Priscilla's stiff posture, the way she clung to her purse as though she were holding onto a lifeline.

"She's lying, you know." The words tumbled out before I could stop them.

"I know." Kade's response was measured, calm. Annoyingly so.

I turned to him fully, my arms crossing. "Why didn't you press her harder?"

"Because pushing someone like Priscilla too far only makes her dig in her heels," he said, his voice even. "She's scared. And scared people either lash out or shut down. I don't need her retreating entirely."

I mulled that over, begrudgingly accepting the logic. Not that I'd admit it. "She's scared for a reason. Whoever's behind this isn't playing nice."

"Agreed." His fingers drummed lightly against the steering wheel, a small, subconscious movement that betrayed his own unease. "But it's not all going to unravel in one interview." He pulled up in front of our place, shifting into park but making no move to turn off the engine. "I've got a briefing at ten— nothing to do with this case. You good to hold down the fort for a bit?"

"Pretty sure I can manage," I said dryly.

"Not worried about being left unsupervised?"

I smirked. "You say that like I haven't already planned my next terrible decision."

Kade shook his head, amusement flickering behind his gaze. "Try not to burn anything down while I'm gone."

I shot him a mock glare. "You married me. You don't get to complain."

Kade smirked, then leaned over, catching my wrist before I could escape. "Come here," he murmured, his voice dropping low enough to make my breath hitch.

Before I could retort with something witty—or at least pretend to—his lips brushed mine, soft and steady, but with that hint of stubborn determination that was so very him. It wasn't long or dramatic, but it was enough to send a pleasant warmth curling through my chest.

"Be good," he said as he pulled back, his hand lingering on my cheek for half a second longer than necessary.

"Where's the fun in that?" I quipped, though my voice came out softer than I intended.

His eyes lingered on mine, a quiet intensity passing between us before he finally let go. "I mean it. Stay out of trouble."

"I'll do my best," I lied, giving him a grin as I

climbed out, shutting the door behind me. As he drove off, I glanced around, half-expecting Ben or Sandra to pop back into existence.

Nothing.

Wherever they'd gone, I had a feeling I'd find out soon enough.

The morning air curled around me, laced with the crisp scent of freshly cut grass. I exhaled, turning toward the house where Thor sat by the door, his plump body radiating impatience. As I stepped onto the porch, he wound between my legs with the precision of a seasoned ankle assassin, his tail flicking against my calf. His gaze met mine—flat, unimpressed, and brimming with judgment.

"I'm starving," he announced, tail twitching. "I've been abandoned for hours, and my bowl is—"

"Full," I interrupted, unlocking the front door and nudging it open. "It's full. It's always full. You're dramatic."

Thor trotted inside ahead of me, his tail high, a furry flag of protest. "Dry food is not a meal. It's an insult."

"Tell that to your vet," I muttered, shutting the door behind me. "She's the one who said you need to cut back."

"I'm big-boned," Thor shot back, leaping onto

the couch and settling in like the king of everything. Ignoring his grumbling, I dropped my bag onto the counter and stood in my office doorway, scanning the room. Delaney Investigations wasn't much—just a cozy, cluttered space that was my home office. But it worked, and it carried Ben's fingerprints everywhere: the old leather chair he'd loved, the dented filing cabinet, even the ghost of a coffee ring on the desk. It was both comforting and bittersweet, a constant reminder of why I was doing this.

Setting my phone on the desk, I checked the time. Kade's briefing would keep him busy for a couple of hours, which meant I had time to work through the million questions still circling my brain. I called out to the empty room. "Ben? You here, or are you off haunting someone more interesting?"

No response.

I wandered into the kitchen, hoping to find him lurking near the fridge—his usual favorite spot for throwing out unsolicited advice. But the kitchen was empty, save for Bandit, who had apparently broken into the pantry—again! She was halfway into a box of cereal, her little hands working methodically to fish out the last of the sugary goodness.

"Bandit!" I yelped, grabbing the box. "How many times? Seriously!"

She chittered at me, scampering up onto the counter with her prize—a single, sad-looking marshmallow. "You weren't eating it. Finders, keepers."

"Unbelievable," I muttered, tossing the box into the pantry and shutting it firmly. "Thor's dramatic, and you're a thief. I'm surrounded by chaos."

"Sorry, Mom," she called over her shoulder, disappearing up the stairs.

I sighed, rubbing the bridge of my nose. "Ben," I tried again, louder this time. "You're freaking me out. Where are you?"

Still nothing. The silence was starting to gnaw at me, settling heavily in my gut. Ben wasn't one to disappear without a good reason. Either he was avoiding me—which was possible, but unlikely—or he was onto something he didn't want me to know about yet.

I returned to the desk, my eyes narrowing at the faint shimmer in the air by the bookshelf. A flicker of movement caught my attention, and finally Ben materialized, looking far too pleased with himself.

"Took you long enough," I said, crossing my arms. "Where have you been?"

He shrugged, leaning against the bookshelf like

he wasn't about to drop something massive on me. "Oh, you know. Around."

"Define 'around.' And it better be good."

Ben's grin widened, and I knew immediately I wasn't going to like whatever he was about to say.

"Let's just say," he began, his tone casual, "that I've been following up on a lead. A big one."

I frowned, suspicion creeping in. "And you didn't think to tell me?"

"Didn't want to get your hopes up," he said, his voice softening slightly. "But I found something, Fitz. Something big."

My heart kicked up a notch. "What kind of something?"

Ben straightened, his grin fading. "You're going to want to sit down for this."

I sank into the old leather chair, my pulse thrumming in my ears. "All right, Casper, spill. What did you find?"

Ben hovered near the desk, his usually relaxed posture suddenly tense. His eyes darted to the living room, where Thor was dramatically sprawled across the couch, clearly uninterested in anything not involving food.

"I've been poking around," Ben started, his tone serious. "Checking in on some... people."

"Ben," I said, leaning forward. "You're killing me here—pun intended. What people? What did you find?"

"Claire Hanover."

The name landed between us, heavy enough to pull my focus into sharp clarity. I frowned. "Claire Hanover? Why are we talking about her now?"

Ben crossed his arms, his expression grim. "Because she's more involved in this mess than we thought. Turns out, she's been hiding a little secret."

I tilted my head, trying to read his face. "Care to elaborate, or are you going to keep me dangling here?"

Ben flickered for a moment—whether from excitement or frustration, I couldn't tell. "She's been having an affair."

I froze, my mind racing. "An affair? With who?"

"That," Ben said, pointing a translucent finger at me, "is the kicker. Daniel Craig."

I blinked again, the pieces of the puzzle rattling in my head. "Ethan Craig's dad? The guy who's been throwing money around like it's Monopoly cash? That Daniel Craig?"

"The very same," Ben confirmed. "And let's just say it's not a secret Claire's keen to get out."

My stomach churned as the implications began

to unravel. "So, let me get this straight. The vice principal of the school is sleeping with a wealthy, married parent. And this has *what* to do with Sandra?"

"Don't know yet," Ben admitted, his voice tinged with frustration. "But I'm betting it's connected. Claire's a key player in all of this, Fitz. She's not as squeaky clean as she looks."

"No kidding," I muttered, running a hand through my hair. "But how does Priscilla fit into this? She said she found the financial records in Claire's office. Was she snooping because she suspected Claire of having an affair or because of something else?"

Ben's eyes narrowed. "That's the million-dollar question. And something tells me Priscilla's not exactly eager to share the whole truth."

I groaned, slumping back in the chair. "Of course she isn't. Why make my life easy when she can make it a soap opera?"

"Speaking of drama," Ben added, his tone lighter now, "you should probably know that Claire's been doing some damage control. I caught her deleting emails on her office computer. And if she's smart, she's already shredding whatever she can get her hands on."

"Well, that's fantastic," I said, my sarcasm in full swing. "Nothing like chasing after a trail that's actively being erased. Guess I know who I'm paying a visit to next," I muttered.

Ben's grin widened as he rubbed his hands together. "Let's rattle some skeletons."

CHAPTER ELEVEN

Grabbing my bag and keys in one swift motion, I made my way toward the front door where Ben stood waiting, arms casually crossed and a wide grin stretched across his face. His eyes sparkled with anticipation as he leaned slightly against the doorframe. "So, what's the plan, boss?" he asked, his voice bubbling with eagerness.

"The plan is to poke the hornet's nest and see what buzzes out," I replied. "You coming?"

"I wouldn't miss it," he said, mock-saluting.

Stepping outside, I tugged my coat tighter around me as the brisk, biting air sliced through the morning, even sharper than it had been earlier. The chill nipped at my skin, but I didn't mind too much

—after all, it wasn't nearly as annoying as the coffee I'd already spilled down the front of my shirt this morning. A perfect start to the day, truly.

I settled into the driver's seat and was about to turn on the engine when it dawned on me—I forgot my phone! "Ugh," I muttered, dragging myself out of the car and heading back inside to grab the phone I'd left on my desk.

"Back already?" Thor mumbled sleepily from the couch.

"Nope, just a figment of your imagination," I muttered, grabbing my phone off the desk before heading out *again*.

This time, I actually made it down the street. The drive to Firefly Bay school was short, and by the time the school came into view, my irritation had morphed into anticipation. The brick facade looked as innocent and ordinary as ever, but I knew better. Firefly Bay school wasn't just a place of ABCs and glitter glue; it was a breeding ground for drama. And Claire Hanover was right at the center of it.

Inside, the pungent scent of disinfectant mingled with the sharp tang of floor polish, creating an olfactory assault that was unmistakably the hallmark of an elementary school. The air was thick with the distinctive aroma of a hundred small bodies, a mix of crayons, glue, and the faint sweetness of childhood. It hit me like a sensory gut-punch, instantly transporting me back to my own school days. Barb, the perpetually cheerful front office receptionist, sat behind the front desk, her fingers a blur of motion as they danced furiously across the keyboard.

"Hi, Barb," I said, flashing her a smile that, if I'm being honest, probably looked a little too eager.

Barb beamed. "Audrey! What brings you by?"

"Is Claire in? I was hoping to have a quick word."

"She's in a meeting," Barb informed me, her eyes flicking briefly to the glowing screen of her computer. "But she should be free soon. Want me to let her know you're waiting?"

"That's okay," I replied, offering a small smile. "I'll wait out here."

I eased myself into one of the hard plastic chairs lined against the wall and pulled out my phone, scrolling aimlessly to appear occupied. Meanwhile, Ben lounged casually against the wall, a mischievous smirk playing on his lips, as if he found amusement in the mundane wait.

"You're not actually waiting, are you?"

"Give it five minutes," I murmured. "Once Barb's distracted, I'm slipping in."

Ben chuckled. "Classic Fitz."

Sure enough, Barb's phone rang a few minutes later, and she answered it with her usual chirpy enthusiasm. I stood and made my way down the hallway, my footsteps echoing against the tiled floor as I kept my pace casual and unhurried. The door to Claire's office was closed—no surprise there—but I had Ben with me, and he was more effective than any lock pick.

"Go on, Casper," I said, motioning to the door. "See if she's hiding anything."

He saluted and disappeared through the door. I leaned against the wall, feigning interest in an outdated fire safety poster, its corners curling slightly with age while my pulse drummed loudly in my ears.

Minutes later, Ben reappeared, his expression grim. "Her computer's clean—too clean. She's been scrubbing files like her life depends on it. But I found her trash folder."

I arched a brow. "And?"

"And she's not as good at deleting things as she thinks she is," he said. "There are traces of emails about payouts. Big ones. And I found a string of messages with Daniel Craig. Let's just say they were... intimate."

I arched a brow. "How intimate?"

He wiggled his eyebrows. "If those emails leaked, they would create a scandal and then some."

Before I could respond, the sharp staccato of heels clicking on the linoleum floor made me straighten up. Claire Hanover rounded the corner with an air of authority, her sharp gaze zeroing in on me like a heat-seeking missile. "Ms. Fitzgerald," she said, her tone polite but tinged with a cautious edge. "What brings you to the school?"

I plastered on my most disarming smile, stretching my lips in a way that I hoped conveyed the right blend of friendliness and professionalism and not—as sometimes happened—a snarl. "Just following up on Sandra Greaves' case. Do you have a moment?" I asked, trying to keep my tone light and conversational.

Her lips pressed into a thin, taut line, a clear indication of her reluctance, yet she nodded. "Step into my office," she replied curtly.

I trailed behind her, maintaining a neutral expression even though my pulse thudded loudly in my ears. Claire's office was immaculate, a testament to her meticulous nature. Not a single paper was out of place, each document aligned perfectly on her polished mahogany desk. The air was tinged with the faint scent of lavender from a discreet diffuser on a shelf. If she was nervous, she concealed it masterfully beneath her composed exterior.

"Please, have a seat," she said, gesturing to a chair.

I sat, pretending not to notice how her fingers tightened slightly around the edge of her desk. "Thanks for taking the time," I said. "I just have a few questions about Sandra's work here."

Claire's smile didn't quite reach her eyes. "Of course. Sandra was a dedicated teacher. Her loss is deeply felt."

"I'm sure," I said. "Did she ever mention anything unusual to you? Concerns about the school or issues with staff?"

Her eyes became sharp slits, her face a mask of steely calm. "Why do you ask?" she demanded, her voice edged with suspicion.

"Just trying to piece things together," I said lightly. "Her death has raised some questions, and I'm following up on leads."

Claire leaned back, her posture rigid. "I'm afraid I can't help you. As far as I'm aware, Sandra didn't have any issues. She was a model employee."

"Right," I said, nodding like that made perfect

sense. "And you're sure she never brought up anything about finances? Discrepancies, maybe?"

Her mask slipped, if only for a fleeting moment, her eyes flashing with a cold, cutting gleam. "Our finances are audited regularly. There are no discrepancies," she asserted, her voice steady yet edged with a hint of defensiveness. "And let me be clear. Sandra was not involved—in any way—with the running of the school, financial or otherwise."

"Of course," I said, holding her gaze. "I'm just covering all my bases. Thanks for clearing that up."

She hesitated, clearly weighing whether to kick me out or play nice. Finally, she asked, "Is there anything else, Ms. Fitzgerald?"

"Well," I said, leaning forward ever so slightly, my gaze steady and curious. "You know how small towns thrive on gossip... whispers have found their way to me. There's talk about professionalism, particularly concerning relationships between teachers and parents. Is that a common occurrence around here?"

Claire's expression froze, her knuckles whitening as she gripped the edge of her desk. "What exactly are you implying?"

I tilted my head, feigning curiosity. "Oh, nothing.

It's just, small-town schools can be a hotbed for… entanglements."

"I assure you," Claire said, her voice sharp enough to cut glass, "this school holds itself to the highest professional standards."

"Of course," I said, flashing an innocent smile. "I had to ask. Hope you understand."

She stood abruptly, signaling that the conversation was over. "If you have further questions, I suggest you make an appointment." She glanced at her watch, her expression cool. "Right now, I have another meeting to attend."

"I just might do that," I said, standing as well. "Thanks for your time, Ms. Hanover."

As I left the office, Ben kept pace beside me, his grin wicked. "Did you see her face? She practically short-circuited."

"Yeah," I muttered, my mind spinning. "She's definitely up to her neck in it. I just don't know if it involves Sandra."

"She's got skeletons," Ben said. "And I'll bet my ghostly good looks one of them is the reason Sandra's dead."

I shoved open the door, my jaw tightening. "We definitely need to dig deeper into Claire Hanover."

Back at Delaney Investigations—also known as the cozy, chaos-filled Galloway-Fitzgerald household—I sank into my chair and kicked off my boots. Ben hovered near the window, arms crossed, his expression unusually contemplative. "You know," he said finally, "Claire's too polished. We know she's hiding something big. All we have to do is crack her."

"Gee, thanks for the expert insight, Sherlock," I muttered, turning to the computer. "The way she reacted, you'd think I accused her of embezzling directly."

"You kind of did, in a roundabout way," Ben pointed out. "And that crack about the staff-parent relationships? Chef's kiss."

"Subtlety is a gift." I grinned.

My inbox chimed with a new email. I clicked it open, my eyes narrowing as I read. It was from Kade, the subject line: *FYI*. Attached was a file labeled *Craig Family Connections*. I downloaded it, scanning the contents.

"Well, well," I said, my eyebrows climbing. "Kade's been busy."

"Anything juicy?" Ben asked, perching on the edge of the desk.

"Let's see." I leaned closer to the screen. "Daniel Craig. Wealthy donor, father of Ethan Craig, the kid who got into a fight with Elliot Carter. Turns out, Ethan's been flagged for behavioral issues more than once, but thanks to Daddy's deep pockets, it's all been swept under the rug."

"Color me shocked," Ben said dryly. "And the Carters?"

"Olivia Carter, single mom, struggling financially. Her son Elliot got expelled after the fight, while Ethan got a slap on the wrist." I leaned back, chewing my lip. "Looks like someone made sure the Carters were compensated—Claire, maybe? Or Daniel? Either way, money changed hands."

Ben tilted his head. "So, we've got a disgruntled teacher, a possibly corrupt vice principal, and a parent with a reputation for throwing cash around to get what he wants. Any guesses on who's pulling the strings?"

"Right now, they all look guilty as hell," I admitted. "Claire's too polished, Daniel's too smooth, and Priscilla's hiding more than she's willing to admit. And Sandra's dead in the middle of all of it."

"Pun intended?" Ben quipped.

"Obviously." I leaned back, staring at the wall as the puzzle pieces swirled in my head. "We need to figure out why Sandra was killed. What did she stumble across that got her silenced? Was it the money? Claire's affair with a parent?"

"Maybe it wasn't just what she found," Ben said, his tone serious. "Maybe it was who she trusted with it."

As I pondered my next move, my phone buzzed on the desk. I picked it up, frowning at the unknown number flashing on the screen.

"Hello?"

A tense silence hung in the air before a voice, twisted and mangled by a cheap voice changer, crackled ominously through the line. "You're getting too close. Back off."

The line went dead before I could respond. I slumped back in my chair, staring at the phone in my hand. The distorted voice still rang in my ears, sending cold prickles down my spine. Threats. Real ones, aimed at me this time. My palms were clammy, and I rubbed them on my jeans.

Ben eyed me from across the room, lips curled in a smirk. "You look like someone just told you the milk's expired right after you chugged it. What's going on?"

I shot him a glare. "Did you hear any of that? Distorted voice, real creep-show vibes. They told me to back off."

Ben's smirk disappeared, replaced by a frown. "Distorted voice? Didn't Priscilla mention getting a call like that? You think it's the same person?"

That pulled me upright. "Priscilla did say that." The dots started connecting in my head fast enough to make me dizzy. "She said they threatened her, told her to hand over the folder to that guy in the alley. And now they're threatening me. It's got to be the same person."

Ben's jaw tightened. "Whoever this is, they're keeping tabs on the case. On who you're talking to. And they don't like you sticking your nose where it doesn't belong."

"That's too bad for them because sticking my nose where it doesn't belong is literally my job description," I said, trying for bravado even as the chill from the call lingered in my chest.

Ben straightened. "Let me take a look at the call log."

I placed the phone on the desk without a word, watching as he placed his palm flat against the screen. His eyes flicked closed, and for a moment, I could've sworn the air in the room got heavier. A faint glow spread from his hand into the device, a shimmer of light that danced over the edges of the phone.

After a few seconds, Ben's eyes snapped open. He pulled his hand back, shaking it like he'd touched a live wire. "Burner phone. Figures."

I groaned. "Can you at least tell where the call was made from?"

His lips twisted in concentration as he tried again, his hand glowing faintly as he dug deeper. "It's pinging from a cell tower near the docks. Not super precise, but it's something."

"The docks?" I said, sitting up straighter. "That's... random."

"Not exactly the vibe for prank callers," Ben agreed. "Or anyone not involved in sketchy business."

I nodded, filing that away for later. "Thanks, Ben. At least we've got a starting point."

"Glad to help," he said, though he still looked distracted.

I narrowed my eyes at him. "What's wrong?"

"Sandra," he admitted. "I haven't seen her since the station. She's missing out on all the progress we're making."

"You think she followed Priscilla? Maybe back to work or home?"

"Could be," Ben said with a shrug. "I'm going to check in on her."

"Do that," I said, glancing at my phone. "And let me know if you find anything else weird."

He gave me a mock salute before fading from view, leaving me alone with my thoughts and a growing sense of unease.

Thor chose that moment to jump onto the desk and stare me down. His eyes were unblinking, silently demanding to be fed.

"Yeah, soon, Buddy, soon," I muttered, scratching his chin. "This case just got a lot messier."

Thor purred faintly, which was about as close to agreement as he ever got. I sighed, picking up my phone again and scrolling through my notes. The docks. A burner phone. Financial shenanigans and a secret affair.

"Piece of cake," I muttered to myself, pulling up Kade's number. Because if I was heading to the docks, I was sure as hell not going alone.

CHAPTER TWELVE

The docks stretched before me, sun-warmed wood creaking beneath my boots, the scent of brine and diesel hanging thick in the air. Boats bobbed lazily at their moorings, their hulls knocking against the piers. Seagulls circled overhead, their cries blending with the murmur of fishermen unloading their catch.

Kade's SUV pulled up near the edge of the lot, and I watched as he climbed out, his expression already set to *serious cop mode*.

I grinned as he approached. "You got here fast. Starting to think you have a tracker on me."

"You keep getting yourself threatened, and I might consider it," he shot back, stopping in front of me. His gaze swept over me, like he was checking for visible signs of distress. "You okay?"

I rocked on my heels. "Better than okay. This is *good* news."

Kade blinked. "Audrey, someone just threatened you."

"Exactly." I threw my arms out. "Which means I'm getting close. Nobody threatens you unless they're scared. This is like the gold star of investigations."

Kade sighed, pinching the bridge of his nose. "You do realize most people would take a death threat as a sign to *back off*, right?"

"Sure. But those people aren't *me*."

"That," he muttered, "is exactly what worries me."

I waved off his concern. "Come on, I wanted you to meet me here because the call Ben traced pinged somewhere in this area. *Right here.* Which means our mystery caller either dumped the phone, or—"

"Or they're still close by," Kade finished grimly, scanning the area. "Great."

"Relax. If they wanted me dead, they would've been less dramatic about it."

"Again, not the reassurance you think it is," he muttered.

Before I could reply, movement caught my eye. A pair of kids—maybe ten or eleven—were walking toward us from the other end of the pier, one of them holding up a phone like it was a prize from a claw machine.

"You have *got* to be kidding me," I whispered.

Kade followed my gaze as the kids stopped near a stack of lobster crates, peering at the phone's screen.

"Dibs on first crack at it," one said.

"No way! You got first dibs on the last one. It's my turn."

I blinked. "I'm sorry. Are these children *regularly* finding discarded phones?"

Kade was already moving. "Let's go talk to them before they accidentally call someone terrifying."

I followed, letting Kade take the lead since he had that whole *official police authority* thing going for him.

"Hey there," Kade said, keeping his tone light. "Mind telling me where you found that?"

The kid with the phone—a lanky boy in a Red Sox cap—squinted up at him. "Uh... the ground?"

His friend, a girl with a frizzy ponytail, elbowed him. "It was over by the pylons," she offered. "Just sitting there. It's a little wet, but it still turns on."

Kade nodded. "That's pretty lucky. Do you mind if I take a look?"

The boy hesitated. "Are we in trouble?"

"No trouble," I said quickly, flashing a smile. "We're just trying to find out who lost it."

The kid studied us both for a second before finally handing over the phone. Kade took it, turning it over in his hand. A cheap burner, cracked screen, no case. Definitely *not* something a local fisherman would leave behind.

I exhaled slowly. "Think we can get anything off it?"

Kade's jaw ticked. "Possibly. But if this was our caller's phone, odds are they already wiped it."

I crossed my arms. "So, we try anyway. Maybe there's something they missed."

Kade studied me for a second, then nodded. "All right. Let's see if this thing still has a pulse."

Kade pressed the power button, and the burner phone's cracked screen flickered to life. The lock screen was blank—no wallpaper, no personal touches. Just a plain white background with a single notification: *1 Missed Call.*

I leaned in. "That from me?"

Kade's head swiveled so fast I heard an audible crack. "Did you call them back?"

"No."

Kade chuckled and turned his attention back to the phone. "No. It's from a private number."

I frowned. "Our mystery caller *had* a mystery caller?"

Kade's mouth tightened. "That's never a good sign."

I turned back to the kids, who were still lingering, their eyes wide with curiosity. "Hey, thanks for handing this over. You two did good."

The girl beamed. "Are we, like, junior detectives now?"

Kade shot me a warning look, and I held back my immediate *hell yes*. Instead, I went with, "Absolutely. But the first rule of being a junior detective is knowing when to walk away from a case."

The boy groaned. "That sounds boring."

"Trust me, your parents will thank us."

That seemed to do the trick, and after a little more prodding from Kade, the kids scurried off, back to whatever questionable hobby led them to regularly find abandoned electronics.

I turned back to Kade. "All right, we need to get into that phone."

He exhaled. "You know what I'm going to say."

"That we should take it back to the station and let the professionals handle it?"

"Yes."

I sighed. "And you know what *I'm* going to say."

"That you have a ghost best friend with a knack for breaking into things?"

I grinned. "See? We *are* learning."

Kade didn't even argue this time. He just handed over the phone. "Fine. Do it. But if this thing explodes, I *will* tell everyone it was your fault."

I clutched my chest dramatically. "The faith you have in me is overwhelming."

"I have faith in *Ben*," he corrected. "You, however, have a habit of attracting chaos."

I gasped. "That is slander."

"*That*," he said, deadpan, "is the most accurate thing I've said all day."

I ignored him and closed my eyes, focusing on summoning Ben. Sometimes it worked, sometimes it didn't. And sometimes it really—*really*—annoyed Ben.

"Message sent," I told Kade. "Now we wait to see if he received it."

Kade crossed his arms, watching me. "I don't love this."

"I know."

"Remind me why I let you talk me into this again?"

I smiled sweetly. "Because you love me and my chaos is charming?"

He exhaled, rubbing a hand over his face. "God help me."

A breeze kicked up, rustling my hair, and a second later, Ben materialized beside me, looking mildly annoyed. "You *owe* me," he announced.

I raised an eyebrow. "What, Sandra giving you a hard time?"

"No, Sandra *disappeared* on me." He ran a hand through his dark hair. "I was following her after the Priscilla thing, and then poof—gone. I checked her house, the school, even the diner. Nada."

I frowned. "That's... weird."

"Tell me about it." Ben eyed the phone in my hand. "Is that what I think it is?"

I nodded, laying it flat on my palm. "We think it belonged to my mystery caller."

Ben squinted at it. "Basic burner. No SIM card. They wiped it, but..." He pressed his palm flat against the screen, his ghostly energy flickering. "Give me a sec."

I turned to Kade while Ben did his thing. "Ben tells me Sandra has disappeared. He can't find her."

Kade frowned, his expression flat. "And?"

I exhaled sharply. "And that's weird. She was hanging around non-stop, and now she's gone?"

Kade shrugged. "Perhaps she's finally moved on."

I scoffed. "Yeah, sure. Right after we started making real progress? That doesn't make sense."

Ben's sudden *ugh* cut me off.

"What?" I asked.

Ben scowled at the phone. "Your mystery caller was *careful*. Wiped most of the logs. But I can confirm this is the phone used to call you, Fitz."

My pulse jumped. "Ben says this is the phone used to call me."

"They were at the docks," Ben confirmed, removing his hand from the phone. "So, unless they swam off into the sunset, they might still be close."

I turned to Kade. "We need to look around."

His jaw was already tight. "Yeah," he said, scanning the docks. "Let's move."

The moment Kade said *let's move*, my adrenaline spiked. Someone had been here—*was* here—and if we were lucky, they hadn't gotten far.

I handed the burner phone to Kade and took a slow scan of the docks. Boats bobbed lazily in the water, their mooring ropes creaking with the current. A few dock workers were scattered around, hauling crates or chatting, oblivious to the fact that a potential criminal had been lurking nearby.

Kade motioned for me to stay close as we moved toward the water.

"I hate to be the one to point this out," I murmured, "but the ocean is *right there*. If our mystery caller didn't want to be found, they could've taken the express exit."

Kade's expression was unreadable. "Or they could still be watching."

That thought sent a shiver down my spine. I pulled my hoodie tighter around me and cast a glance over my shoulder. No obvious lurkers. But then again, whoever made that call had already proven they were smart.

Ben drifted a few steps ahead, scanning the area with narrowed eyes. "No ghostly residue," he muttered.

I arched an eyebrow. "Ghostly residue?"

He shot me a look. "You know, that weird *leftover* energy spirits sometimes leave behind? It's a thing."

I hummed. "Sounds made up."

"Says the woman with a talking cat and a raccoon that shoplifts."

Fair point.

Kade stopped near a set of wooden stairs leading

down to a lower dock, his gaze sweeping the water. "If they were here, they either ran or hid."

I scanned the boats again, my gut twisting. "Or they're *on* one of those boats."

Kade followed my gaze, his frown deepening. "You think they're still close?"

Before I could answer, Ben suddenly stiffened. His form flickered—just for a second—before he jerked his head toward the far end of the docks. "Someone's moving back there."

Kade and I exchanged a glance as I repeated what Ben had said. Then, without hesitation, we took off. The wooden planks of the dock rattled under our steps as we jogged toward the far end. The scent of salt and engine oil thickened the air, and as we neared a row of smaller boats, I caught movement—a shadow ducking behind a stack of lobster traps.

"There!" I hissed.

Kade moved fast, cutting ahead while I circled wide, trying to flank them. I reached for my phone, ready to snap a picture, when—A figure bolted.

"Stop!" Kade shouted.

Spoiler: They did not stop.

I was already moving, feet pounding against the dock as I gave chase. The figure was smaller than I expected—lean, fast, and dressed in dark clothes that blurred with the shadows.

Ben popped up beside me, floating effortlessly as I gasped for air. "I hate to break it to you, but you are *not* built for sprinting."

"Shut up," I wheezed.

Ahead, Kade was gaining ground, closing the gap. The runner veered toward a fishing boat, leaping onto the deck with the kind of agility I did *not* possess. Kade followed, landing solidly on board, but by the time I scrambled after them, all I caught was a blur of motion—the figure dove over the side of the boat. My breath caught. I skidded to the edge, just in time to see a splash below.

Kade swore. "Damn it."

Ben hovered beside me, watching the ripples in the water. "Well, they're committed."

I groaned. "Who *does* that? Who just *jumps into the ocean*?"

Kade ran a hand through his hair, scanning the water for any sign of our escapee. "Someone who doesn't want to be caught."

I exhaled sharply, frustration tightening my chest. We'd gotten so close. Whoever that was, they had something to hide—and now they were *gone*.

Ben crossed his arms. "Well, that was dramatic."

Kade turned back to me, his expression unreadable. "You okay?"

I huffed. "Yeah. Just annoyed. They were *right there.*"

A shout echoed from down the dock. One of the fishermen had spotted the splash and was pointing, but by the time we looked, there was nothing but open water.

Gone.

Kade clenched his jaw. "We need to figure out who they are."

I nodded, forcing my breath to steady. "And why they called me?"

And more importantly—what they were willing to *kill* to keep hidden.

CHAPTER THIRTEEN

I placed the burner phone on my desk and stared at it like it might spontaneously start confessing its secrets if I glared hard enough. Kade had handed it over reluctantly, making me promise I wouldn't do anything "stupid" with it before he left for the station. Which, honestly, felt insulting. I *never* did stupid things. Ill-advised? Maybe. Boldly reckless? Sure. But stupid? Absolutely not.

Ben stood beside me, arms crossed, watching me with the kind of exhausted patience usually reserved for parents of hyperactive toddlers. "You know I already checked that, right?"

I sighed dramatically, turning to him. "Humor me. What if you missed something?"

Ben scoffed. "I don't *miss* things. I'm a *ghost*. I can literally *touch* the code."

"Yeah, yeah, spectral hacker extraordinaire. Just take another look." I pushed the phone toward him.

He gave me a long-suffering look before plopping a translucent hand onto the device. The screen flickered to life, casting an eerie glow across his already ethereal features. "Wiped clean, just like before," he said, his voice flat.

"Right, but—"

"No contacts, no messages, no call history," he continued, ignoring me. "Just a bunch of sad, empty folders."

I waved a hand impatiently. "Come on, there's *always* something. No one's that good at covering their tracks."

Ben lifted a brow. "*I'm* that good."

I narrowed my eyes. "Well, lucky for us, our mystery villain isn't *you*. Now look harder."

He sighed and muttered something under his breath about "nagging PIs" before his fingers ghosted over the phone's surface again. For a long moment, nothing happened. Then—"Huh."

I perked up. "Huh? What huh? That was a *suspiciously* interesting huh."

He frowned at the screen. "There's a fragment of a text. Partial, but readable."

My pulse kicked up a notch. "What does it say?"

Ben tilted his head, reading aloud. "Meet at usual spot. 8PM."

I straightened, mind spinning. "That's it?"

"That's it," he confirmed. "No sender, no recipient." He hesitated, then added, "If I had to guess? This was sent *to* the burner phone."

Which meant whoever had this phone was meeting someone. And since they'd gone to the trouble of dumping it, they didn't want a record of that meeting.

I tapped my fingers on the desk. "Any way to figure out *who* sent it?"

Ben sighed like I'd asked him to recite *War and Peace* from memory. "It's possible. If Kade can get his hands on cell tower records for this area, I might be able to trace what number pinged this phone."

My excitement was dampened by the realization that this required *cooperating* with the police. "Great. So now I have to convince Kade to play along."

Ben smirked. "Or you could just break into the station and—"

"No."

He sighed dramatically. "You're *so* boring now that you're married."

I rolled my eyes. "Says the *dead* guy."

He grinned, then flickered slightly, his expression shifting. "Speaking of weird things, still no sign of Sandra."

That sobered me up fast.

I sat forward. "Still?"

Ben shook his head. "After the Priscilla thing, she just *vanished*. I checked her house, the school, the diner—nothing. It's like she's avoiding me."

A cold pit settled in my stomach. "You don't think she's... stuck somewhere, do you?"

Ben tilted his head. "What, like *ghost jail?*"

I huffed. "I don't know! I just—she seemed so determined to follow Priscilla, and now she's gone? It doesn't add up."

Ben didn't look convinced. "Sometimes ghosts get *unstable* right before they cross over."

"Yeah, but Sandra hasn't solved her murder yet," I pointed out. "That means she *shouldn't* be crossing over."

He sighed, rubbing the back of his neck. "I'll keep looking, but I don't love this."

"Me neither." I exhaled, glancing back at the phone. "All right, let's focus. If the person who called me is the same one who threatened Priscilla, then we're dealing with someone who *knows a lot.*"

Ben's eyes darkened. "Yeah. And they're getting desperate."

The room felt too quiet after Ben's ominous *they're getting desperate.* The weight of those words settled in my chest. Someone had threatened me. That wasn't new—being a private investigator came with its fair share of pissed-off people—but this wasn't just some angry spouse or a disgruntled fraudster.

This was a murderer. And I was in their way. I let out a slow breath, rolling my shoulders, shaking off the unease. "Let's assume this meeting was *important.* We have a time—8PM. But where's the usual spot?"

"Could be anywhere. If they were careful enough to use a burner, they wouldn't have left an obvious trail," Ben said.

I frowned. "Yeah, but they still had to communicate. If this phone was wiped, what about the *other* phone? The one that sent the message?"

Ben's eyes flickered with something mischievous. "Now *that's* an interesting thought. If we can find the number that texted this phone..."

"We might be able to trace it back to the sender."

I shot him a grin. "See, this is why we work well together. I think of the brilliant ideas, and you do the illegal hacking."

Ben smirked. "You say *illegal*, I say *efficient*." He glanced at the burner phone again, then sighed. "Problem is, I can't do much without access to the actual tower data."

Which meant… Kade.

I leaned back in my chair, staring at the ceiling. "You know how hard it is to get Kade to do shady things for me?"

Ben laughed. "You married a *cop*, Audrey."

"I married a *hot* cop," I corrected. "Big difference."

"And yet, here you are, about to ask him to bend the law."

I folded my arms. "I like to think of it as a *light stretch* rather than a full bend."

Ben shook his head, his amusement giving way to something more serious. "Look, if we're really thinking this is the same person who threatened Priscilla… that means they're watching. They know we're getting close."

The chill that ran down my spine had nothing to do with ghosts. I rubbed my arms, glancing at the burner phone again. "Which means I need to talk to Kade sooner rather than later."

Ben inclined his head toward the door. "Want me to stick around?"

"No," I said automatically. "I can handle this."

I expected an argument, but Ben just studied me for a long moment before nodding. "All right. I'll keep looking for Sandra." And just like that, he was gone.

I exhaled, staring at the now-empty space where he'd stood, then grabbed my jacket and the burner phone. Time to go convince my husband to commit minor police misconduct.

I found Kade at the station, standing outside his office, deep in conversation with Neal McClain. The moment he saw me, his brow furrowed, and he murmured something to Neal before striding toward me.

"You okay?" he asked, scanning me like I might be hiding a bullet wound.

"Fine," I said, waving off his concern. "You got a minute?"

He glanced over his shoulder, then nodded, leading me into his office and shutting the door behind us. "What's going on?"

I pulled the burner phone from my pocket and held it up. "Ben found something. It turns out there was a deleted message. It said 'meet at usual spot, 8PM.'"

Kade's expression darkened. "Sent *to* the burner?"

I nodded.

He exhaled sharply, running a hand through his hair. "All right. What are you thinking?"

"That we need to find out *who* sent that message," I said. "And to do that, we need cell tower data."

Kade gave me a long, unreadable look. "You're asking me to pull private records."

"I'm asking you to *help solve a murder.*"

He sighed, leaning against his desk, arms crossed. "Audrey, I can't access that data without cause."

I took a step closer, lowering my voice. "Someone *threatened me,* Kade. Whoever called Priscilla used a distorted voice. Whoever called me *also* used a distorted voice. That's not a coincidence."

His jaw clenched. "You should've told me that earlier."

"I was *going to.*"

He studied me for a long moment, then finally exhaled. "Okay. Let me see what I can do."

Relief flooded through me, but I kept my expression neutral. "Thanks."

He pushed off his desk and stepped closer, his gaze softening a fraction. "You sure you're okay?"

"I mean, I've been threatened with murder, chased by ghosts, and now I'm asking my husband to flirt with a felony. So, yeah. Totally fine."

His lips twitched. "Come here."

I let him pull me into a hug, my head resting against his chest. For a few precious seconds, I let myself relax.

But then the moment passed, and I stepped back. "I'll keep digging on my end. Let me know what you find."

Kade nodded. "You be careful."

I shot him a grin. "Always."

And with that, I walked out of his office, my mind already spinning with the next steps.

CHAPTER FOURTEEN

There are two things I can always count on at Fitzgerald family dinners:

The food will be excellent.

Someone will ask me when I'm having kids, and I will have to resist the urge to fake a medical emergency to escape.

The moment Kade and I stepped through the front door of my parents' house, we were met with the usual sounds of organized chaos—laughter, the clatter of dishes, and the distinct, high-pitched squeal of a toddler hitting a decibel level that could shatter glass.

"About time you two showed up," Laura called from the kitchen, balancing a wriggling Grace on her hip while stirring a pot of what smelled like her famous mac and cheese. "We were starting to think you got lost."

Kade leaned down to murmur in my ear. "We could still make a run for it."

"I heard that," Laura said over her shoulder. Brad, Laura's husband, grinned at us from his spot at the dining table, where he was attempting to keep Isabelle entertained with a coloring book. "Save yourselves," he said under his breath as Isabelle threw a crayon at him.

Before I could properly assess the battlefield that was family dinner night, my mom swooped in, kissing my cheek and then Kade's. "I'm so glad you made it!"

Pat Fitzgerald was the kind of woman who could convince you that everything was going to be okay with just one look, a trait that I definitely did not inherit. "Come in, come in! Dinner's almost ready."

Dad appeared behind her, giving Kade one of those approving nods that still had an underlying *hurt-my-daughter-and-I'll-bury-you* message. "Kade. Good to see you."

"You too, sir," Kade replied, ever polite.

Dad snorted. "You've been married for three months now. You can stop calling me sir."

Kade smiled. "I don't think I can."

I elbowed him lightly. "See? I married a respectful man. You should be thrilled."

"I *am* thrilled," Dad said, reaching past me to grab a beer from the fridge. "I just think he's trying to make me feel old."

"That ship sailed *years* ago, Dad," Dustin said, strolling in with Amanda by his side. He immediately made a beeline for the chips and dip, ignoring our mother's disapproving glare.

Amanda, dressed in a perfectly pressed cream blouse and navy pencil skirt—because casual family dinners were apparently business casual affairs for her—gave me a quick once-over before offering a smile. "Audrey, how are you? Still getting by without breaking any bones?"

Ah, there it was. The traditional *let's fix Audrey* opening line. Kade slid a hand onto the small of my back in a way that clearly said, *don't take the bait.*

"I'm doing great, actually," I said, keeping my tone light. "I only tripped twice this week, so I'm practically a professional athlete at this point."

Amanda hummed like she wasn't convinced. "I still think you should consider getting tested for dyspraxia. There are great specialists—"

"I *love* this conversation," I interrupted, reaching for a roll. "But what I love even more is *not* talking about how I walk like a baby deer on ice. Kade, help me out here?"

Kade, bless him, didn't even hesitate. "Amanda, you *do* know Audrey once managed to trip over *air*, right?"

Dustin snickered into his beer. "Oh, I remember. That was Christmas three years ago. She was standing completely still and then boom —floor."

"That floor came out of nowhere," I muttered.

Madeline, Dustin, and Amanda's five-year-old, looked up from her coloring page. "Auntie Audrey, you should be more careful."

"Thank you for that, Mads."

"Do you want me to hold your hand?" she asked, very seriously.

I sighed dramatically. "Yes, please. At least someone here is looking out for me."

Dinner was called before Amanda could push the dyspraxia conversation any further, and we all shuffled to the table. I took my usual spot between Kade and Isabelle, who immediately clutched my sleeve.

"After dinner, can we play princesses?"

"You know I take my princessing very seriously," I told her. "What's the mission?"

She pondered for a moment, then said, "We have to rescue Sir Fluffybottom."

"I assume he's been kidnapped?"

"Yes! By a dragon."

"Well, that's unfortunate. But I think we can handle it."

Kade nudged me. "I like how you're just accepting that this is happening."

"Of course it's happening," I said. "Sir Fluffybottom is in *danger*."

Laura beamed at me like I'd won big sister points. "You are a good aunt."

I preened. "I *am* the favorite."

"Hey!" Dustin and Amanda complained in unison. Mom shook her head and started passing around the dishes. "Eat before it gets cold."

Dinner was the usual blend of food, laughter, and interruptions from small children. At some point, Grace flung a spoonful of mashed potatoes directly at Kade, who dodged it like the trained professional he was. Dustin tried to start a debate about football. Brad attempted to talk about his latest fishing trip, and through it all, Amanda kept throwing subtle but pointed glances in my direction. I knew what was coming before she even opened her mouth.

"So, Audrey," Amanda said, cutting into her roasted chicken with a practiced hand. "Now that you and Kade are settled, have you given any thought to starting a family?"

The table fell *dead silent.*

I gripped my fork. This was it. This was the moment. Kade's hand found mine under the table and gave it a squeeze. A quiet *I've got you.*

"Well," I said, forcing a smile. "That's an interesting question." And that's when Isabelle, bless her little heart, took matters into her own hands.

"Can we have ice cream?" she asked, completely derailing the conversation.

I leaned down and whispered, "I will buy you all the ice cream in the world." She nodded solemnly, like we had made an unbreakable pact. And just like that, family dinner continued as if nothing had happened. But I knew Amanda wouldn't let it go. And, truth be told, neither would I.

The drive home was quiet at first. The kind of quiet that wasn't uncomfortable but wasn't exactly easy, either. The headlights cut through the darkness, the occasional flicker of a streetlamp casting shadows across Kade's face as he kept his eyes on the road. One hand rested on the wheel, the other on my knee, his thumb moving in slow, absentminded circles against my jeans.

I stared out the window, watching the houses blur past, pretending like my brain wasn't replaying every single comment from dinner.

Kade cleared his throat. "You want to talk about it?"

I turned to look at him, feigning confusion. "Talk about what?"

He glanced at me, one brow arching in the way that said *Really?*

I sighed, stretching out my legs. "Fine. If you're referring to *the baby talk*—" I made air quotes around the words, "—then no. I don't need to talk about it. Because it's not a thing."

"It's not a thing?" he echoed, amused. "You're sure? Because it seemed like a *thing* when Amanda was trying to organize our reproductive schedule over roast chicken."

I made a face. "She does love a well-laid plan."

Kade hummed in agreement. "So... you haven't thought about it?"

My mouth opened, then closed. My first instinct was to give a quick, *Nope. Not even a little bit.* But that was a lie. Of *course* I'd thought about it. Just... not in the way everyone seemed to *want* me to.

"I love kids," I said instead, my voice careful. "I love *our* nieces and nephews. I love playing princess rescue missions and getting sticky hugs and even listening to Isabelle explain, in detail, why the moon is her favorite shape."

"But..." Kade prompted, his voice gentle.

I swallowed. My fingers found the seam of my jeans, tracing it idly. "It's not the having kids part that freaks me out."

Kade didn't say anything, just let the words sit between us, waiting for me to keep going. I exhaled, my heart thudding a little harder than it should have. "It's the *getting-them-here* part." The words felt too big and too small all at once, but they were out now, floating in the space between us.

Kade's fingers tightened slightly on my knee, his warmth steady and solid. "Because of Grace's birth?"

I let out a humorless laugh. "Ya think?"

He didn't push. Just waited.

I licked my lips, staring out at the road. "I was there, Kade. I *saw* it. I saw my sister, who is a literal *warrior* of a woman, in *pain*—like, *real* pain. And I was *powerless* to help her." My throat tightened. "And then there was Grace—this tiny, beautiful, screaming thing, and suddenly everything was fine, but for hours it *wasn't* fine. And I couldn't stop thinking—what if it wasn't? What if something went wrong? What if I—"

I stopped. Shook my head.

Kade didn't rush to fill the silence.

Eventually, I huffed out a breath and forced a smile. "I know, I know. People have babies every day. Women have been doing it forever. Some even like it. Yay for them." I waved a hand. "But I also know that I suck at pain and that my track record with *normal bodily functions* is *not good*. My own limbs *betray* me on a daily basis. Do you really think my body is suddenly going to become *competent* at pushing a whole human out of me?"

Kade's lips twitched. "I mean, I think your body would know what to do."

"Debatable."

He chuckled, but the amusement didn't reach his eyes. He gave my knee another squeeze. "You don't have to convince me, Audrey. If you're not ready, you're not ready. And if you *never* want kids, I need you to know that's okay, too."

Something in my chest squeezed. "You say that now, but what if one day you change your mind?"

His hand slid from my knee to my fingers, lacing them together. "Then I'll change my mind *with* you. But right now? The only thing I care about is you not being afraid. Because if the idea of having a baby is *this* scary for you, then maybe we're not meant to be thinking about it right now."

I chewed my lip. "What if I never stop being scared?"

He smiled at me then, small but sure. "Then we'll cross that bridge when we get to it."

I blew out a breath, tension easing from my shoulders. We drove the rest of the way home in silence, Kade's fingers still tangled with mine, his thumb running small, lazy circles over my skin.

Maybe I'd never want kids. Maybe I'd change my mind. Maybe I'd wake up one day and suddenly *not* feel like childbirth was an exorcism-level nightmare scenario.

I didn't know.

But right now?

Right now, I was really, really grateful that Kade wasn't in any hurry to figure it out.

The house was dark when Kade and I got home, but I wasn't ready to call it a night. My mind was still buzzing from dinner, from the baby talk, from the case. I settled at my desk, clicking on my computer monitor, when a sudden chill crept up my spine.

Sandra's ghost materialized in the corner of the room. Not flickering, not fading—just *wrong*. Like something inside her had been jostled loose, and she was still trying to find her balance.

I jerked back, startled. Not because she was a ghost—I was used to that—but because I'd never seen her like this before. Her usual poise had crumbled, replaced by something raw and unsettled. Her hands fidgeted at her sides, her chest rising and falling in quick, shallow breaths—a pointless mimicry of panic.

"Sandra?" I frowned. "Where the hell have you been?"

She swallowed hard, fingers clenching. "I was at the school."

Something about the way she said it sent a shiver down my spine. I shifted forward, wary. "And?"

"I—I don't know," she stammered, her voice too thin, too uncertain. "I was just *there*, and then... I heard things. I *felt* things." She exhaled sharply, shaking her head as if trying to physically shake off the lingering sensation. "I thought it was happening in real-time, but now—I'm not sure."

A deeper cold settled over me. Ghosts didn't hallucinate. Not like this.

"Start from the beginning," I said, keeping my voice steady. "What happened?"

Sandra shook her head, frustration tightening

her features. "I was drawn there. I don't know how else to explain it. I was just... *pulled* into it. One second I was standing in the hallway, and then—" She swallowed. "I heard voices."

A door slammed somewhere in the house— Kade moving around, probably grabbing a beer before heading to bed. I barely registered it. My focus was locked on Sandra.

"What voices?" I pressed.

Her gaze darted around the room, her fingers curling into the fabric of her cardigan. "A man and a woman. They were arguing."

My pulse quickened. "Do you remember what they said?"

She squeezed her eyes shut. "I think... I think it was about me."

I stiffened. "What do you mean?"

Sandra's voice dropped to a whisper. "The man said something like, 'You should've never talked to her.'" Her expression twisted, as though she were trying to pull the memory back from the depths of her mind. "And the woman—she was crying. Saying she didn't mean to. That it wasn't supposed to happen."

A slow, creeping dread curled through my

stomach. "What wasn't supposed to happen?" I whispered.

Sandra's eyes snapped open, her frustration crackling through the air like static. "I *don't know!* It's like trying to remember a dream—it's slipping away as soon as I grab onto it."

She dragged a hand down her face before exhaling sharply. "But I *felt* it, Audrey. Like I was there, standing in that moment, not just watching it."

I opened my mouth to press her further, but then —Ben popped into existence beside her. "There you are," he grumbled, giving Sandra a once-over before turning to me. "I checked the school again. She wasn't there."

Sandra blinked at him. "Of course I wasn't. I left. I came here."

Ben frowned, rubbing his jaw. "Have you been doing that all day? Popping in and out all over the place? Because every time I looked for you, you weren't there."

Sandra huffed. "I *didn't* pop back like nothing happened. I *felt* something. I was *somewhere*. I just —" She cut herself off, pressing her fingers to her temple. "I don't know."

I frowned. "Could it have been a memory?

Something buried so deep you didn't even realize it was there?"

Sandra let out a frustrated sigh. "Perhaps? But I don't feel like it was *mine*. It felt... recent. Like I was overhearing something."

Ben tapped his fingers against the desk. "So, what, you ghost-eavesdropped? And now the details are slipping away?"

Sandra shot him a look. "I don't need the sarcasm."

I held up a hand. "Okay, let's not bicker. We need to work with what we *do* know. A man and a woman were arguing. The guy said she shouldn't have talked to *her*—which could mean you, Sandra, or someone else entirely."

Sandra nodded. "And the woman sounded upset. Regretful."

"That could be guilt," I mused. "Or fear."

Ben pulled a face. "So... was it a memory or something else? Because this sounds more like reliving than remembering."

I turned back to Sandra. "We'll figure it out. But first—I need you to tell me everything else you remember. No detail is too small."

She nodded, though her frustration still simmered beneath the surface. "Okay. I'll try."

CHAPTER FIFTEEN

$\mathcal{T}$he morning arrived too soon, dragging me out of a restless sleep filled with half-formed theories and Sandra Greaves' ghostly frustration echoing in my skull. The case was a knotted mess, and no amount of sleep was helping untangle it.

Kade had already left for work, leaving behind a fresh cup of coffee on my nightstand because he was the best husband ever. I made a mental note to kiss him properly later.

In the kitchen, Thor was parked beside his food bowl, staring at it like he could will more kibble into existence. Bandit was nowhere to be seen, which was an immediate red flag. I found her seconds later, crouched on the counter, happily munching on the corner of my toast.

"Seriously?" I snatched it back, but she just licked her little raccoon fingers and gave me an unapologetic stare. "I live with criminals."

Thor flicked his tail. "And yet, I'm the one on a diet."

I ignored his judgment and focused on the more pressing issue: Sandra.

Ben materialized in the chair across from me, looking as fresh as an undead daisy. "She's still at her apartment. Hasn't moved since last night."

I set my coffee down. "So, she just... gave up?"

He shrugged. "Frustration. Probably exhaustion. Turns out, not remembering how you died is stressful."

"Well, that makes two of us," I muttered. "Did she say anything before she left?"

"Nothing useful. Just kept saying she *knew* she was missing something but couldn't force it to surface. Then she bailed."

"Did you see anyone else while you were watching her place?"

"Nope. A whole lot of nothing." Ben stretched his legs out, eyeing my toast like he was considering attempting to eat it. "What's next?"

I scrubbed a hand over my face, still not fully awake. "Next, I'm going to pay Olivia Carter a visit."

Ben raised an eyebrow. "You're going in alone?"

"Kade's at work, and I don't need backup." I picked up my coffee, taking a fortifying sip. "Olivia's not a threat. She's a mom who got thrown into a mess because her son was expelled, and Daniel Craig's a manipulative jackass."

"True," Ben admitted. "But that doesn't mean she'll be happy to see you."

"I'm not expecting hugs and baked goods," I said dryly. "I just need to get a read on her. She might not even know she was part of something potentially illegal."

Ben steepled his fingers and rested his chin on them, considering. "Does Olivia know the money came from Claire specifically, or does she think it was from the school as a whole?"

"That's what I'm going to find out." I grabbed my keys and slipped on my jacket. "You sticking with Sandra?"

Ben gave me a lazy salute. "Yeah. Just in case she remembers something useful."

I nodded. "Good. And keep an eye out for anything weird."

Ben smirked. "Define 'weird' in a town where

you talk to ghosts, your cat complains about his diet, and a raccoon just stole your breakfast."

I shot Bandit a glare. She waved a sticky paw at me, utterly unbothered.

Ben vanished, leaving me to head out on my own.

Olivia Carter lived in a tidy, single-story house on the quiet side of town. The kind of place where every lawn was neatly trimmed, and people still brought their trash cans in the same day as collection.

I rang the doorbell and took a step back, hands in my jacket pockets. The door opened a crack, revealing a cautious brown eye peering out.

"Mrs. Carter?"

She hesitated, then opened the door a little wider. "Yes?"

I kept my voice even. "I'm Audrey Fitzgerald. Private investigator. I wanted to ask you a few questions about Elliot's expulsion."

Her expression shifted—wariness, maybe a flicker of curiosity. "That was months ago. What does it matter now?"

"I know it wasn't fair. Elliot took the fall while Ethan Craig walked away clean."

That got her attention. Her posture stiffened, but she didn't slam the door in my face. Small victories.

"I'd like to hear your side," I added. "If you're willing."

She studied me for a moment longer, then exhaled sharply and stepped back. "Fine. Come in."

The inside of the house was as neat as the outside, but there were signs of life—a pile of laundry waiting to be folded, a couple of school books left on the coffee table. Olivia motioned for me to sit, but she remained standing, arms crossed over her chest.

"I don't know what you expect me to say," she said. "That whole mess was last year."

I settled into the chair, watching her carefully. "I just want to understand what happened."

Her arms tightened. "Elliot didn't start that fight."

I nodded. "I believe you."

That threw her off. Just a little.

Her fingers twisted together, her expression caught somewhere between frustration and resignation. "Elliot's attendance was already a miracle. We only got in because of the scholarship program—one of those 'local family, bright future' things they trot out for good PR. It covered most of the tuition, but there were conditions. Behavioral expectations. Academic benchmarks. One screw-up, and the scholarship was gone."

"So the fight wasn't just about the fight," I said softly. "It was about losing everything."

Olivia's jaw tightened. "I begged them to reconsider. Pointed out that Ethan started it. But they didn't care. Elliot was the scholarship kid. The easy one to cut loose."

I stayed quiet, waiting.

She huffed out a bitter breath. "Claire tried to help me. She really did. But the board wouldn't have it." A pause. "My friendship with Claire stood for nothing."

There it was. My head tilted slightly. "You and Claire are friends?"

She blinked, like she hadn't meant to say that. Her fingers twisted together. "Yeah. We met through the school. Talked a lot. Had coffee, that sort of thing." A quick shrug. "We were close, I guess."

I filed that away. *Claire wasn't just some school official to Olivia—she was a friend.*

"And then?" I prompted.

Olivia's mouth tightened. "And then Elliot got expelled, and Claire did nothing to stop it."

"Nothing?"

"She told me she fought for him," Olivia said. "That she tried to argue his case to the board. But when they refused, that was it. She just... let it happen."

I tapped my fingers lightly against my knee. "So, you felt betrayed."

She didn't answer, which was an answer in itself. I let a beat pass, then asked, "Did you ever consider suing?"

She blinked at me. "No."

"But you were angry."

"Of course I was angry," she snapped, then immediately reined herself in. "But a lawsuit? Against the school? That would have been impossible."

"Because they had more resources?"

She gave a short, humorless laugh. "Because Daniel Craig made sure I knew I didn't have a chance."

I kept my face neutral, my pulse kicking up. "Daniel Craig spoke to you about it?"

She hesitated, then let out a slow breath. "Yeah."

"What did he say?"

"He showed up at my house," she admitted. "Acted like he just wanted to talk. Said he understood how hard it was for me, but that this was the best outcome for everyone."

"And when you pushed back?"

She exhaled sharply. "He said things would get 'messy' if I didn't accept it." Her fingers dug into her sleeves. "That the school had already made its decision, and I'd regret making trouble."

I kept my expression smooth, but my teeth clenched. Daniel Craig didn't just pull strings—he strangled people with them.

Olivia looked down at the floor. "I knew what he was saying. That if I tried to fight it, they'd find a way to make my life hell."

I let the silence stretch before asking, "And then, sometime after that, you received a payout."

She flinched, her head snapping up. "What does that have to do with anything?"

I shrugged. "I just want to understand how it happened."

Her arms tightened across her chest again. "Claire told me the board approved it."

"Before or after the money arrived?"

She hesitated. "After."

Another crack.

"You never requested it?"

She shook her head. "I was upset, obviously. I told people I was going to fight back, but I never actually hired a lawyer. Didn't even know where to start." A pause. "Then, out of nowhere, a settlement appeared."

I watched her carefully. "Did you sign anything?"

She frowned. "No."

And there it was. If it had been a real settlement, there would have been paperwork. A formal agreement. Instead, Claire had quietly funneled the money into Olivia's account and only afterward told her it was a board-approved payout.

I let the moment stretch. "That's... unusual."

Olivia swallowed. "Are you saying the board didn't approve it?"

I shook my head. "I don't know. But you didn't sign anything, and there's no record of a negotiation." I lifted a shoulder. "That's not typically how settlements work."

She exhaled shakily. "But Claire told me—"

"Claire told you after the money was already in your account," I said gently.

Her face tightened. She wasn't ready to say it out loud, but I could see the thoughts racing behind her eyes. She had never questioned it before. Never had a reason to. Now she did.

I slid a card onto the table. "If you remember anything—anything at all—call me."

She stared at it, turning it over in her fingers. "I don't know if I can help."

"You already have."

For the second time in twenty-four hours, I stood outside Claire Hanover's office, pretending I belonged there.

I knocked once and stepped inside before she could tell me not to. She was seated behind her desk, a portrait of control—everything in its place, no loose papers, no mess. She didn't like disorder. It made people like her nervous.

She glanced up, already looking like she wanted me gone. "Ms. Fitzgerald. What a surprise."

I smiled. "I had an interesting chat with Olivia Carter this morning."

Claire's expression didn't change, but the pause before she answered was just noticeable enough. "Oh?"

"She told me about the money she received after Elliot's expulsion."

A flicker of something passed through her gaze before she settled into a carefully neutral look. "I see."

I gave her a moment to say something. She didn't. "Thing is," I continued, "she never requested a payout. Never signed anything. One day, the money was just there."

Claire let out a slow breath, a picture of patience. "The board wanted to avoid unnecessary escalation."

That was interesting. "So, the board approved it?"

A second too long before she said, "It was in everyone's best interest."

That wasn't an answer. I cocked my head, watching her closely. "I imagine there would be records of that decision. Meeting minutes. A vote."

She smiled. "Those kinds of records aren't made available to the public."

Still not a yes. I let that sit before shifting tactics. "Olivia said you fought for Elliot to stay."

Claire's fingers twitched before she clasped them together again. "I did."

"She also said you were friends."

That got a reaction. Her lips pressed together, just slightly. "I tried to help her," she said after a moment. "But the board had already made up its mind."

"And after she lost that fight, money appeared in her account."

Her expression smoothed out. "It was a resolution." That was the second time she had dodged saying the board approved it.

I leaned back, keeping my tone casual. "It's unusual for settlements to happen without any paperwork."

She didn't blink. "It was handled appropriately."

"Right. And Olivia never gave the school her banking details, so how did the payment get arranged?"

That one landed. Just for a second. Then she recovered, folding her hands neatly on the desk. "I assume the finance department took care of it."

I nodded like that made perfect sense. I stood, slipping my hands into my pockets. "Thanks for clearing that up."

She watched me carefully. "Of course."

I turned for the door, then paused, looking back. "One more thing. If I wanted to verify the board's approval, who would I need to speak with?"

She didn't move.

"There would be no need for that," she said finally.

I smiled. "Right. Because it's all in the records."

Another pause.

"Have a good afternoon, Ms. Fitzgerald."

I walked out, my pulse picking up. Claire hadn't denied it. She hadn't confirmed it either, but that was almost worse.

CHAPTER SIXTEEN

I sat in my car, drumming my fingers against the steering wheel, watching the entrance of the school. Claire Hanover had been composed—too composed. But beneath that icy veneer, she was cracking. The way she sidestepped my questions, the tension in her jaw when I mentioned Olivia Carter, the absolute shutdown when I asked about verifying the board's approval— it all pointed to one thing.

She was in trouble. And she knew it.

The problem was, I still didn't have enough to nail her. I had Ben's word that she'd funneled school money into Olivia's account. I had her careful deflections, and I had Olivia's testimony, but I needed *proof*. Something irrefutable. Something that would make Claire or the board start talking.

A movement near the entrance caught my eye.

Claire.

She was moving fast, all business, except there was something about the way she kept glancing around that wasn't business as usual. She practically launched herself into her car and slammed the door.

I straightened. *Where are you going in such a hurry?*

Her engine roared to life, and before I could second-guess myself, I started mine, too. The trick to tailing someone without being obvious? Act like you belong.

Claire peeled out of the parking lot, and I followed at a casual pace, keeping two cars between us. Claire didn't go home. She didn't go to a restaurant or a bar or anywhere that suggested a meeting that could be explained away. She pulled into a motel. That was when I knew I was about to hit gold.

I rolled past the entrance and pulled into the diner across the street, choosing a spot that gave me a perfect view of the parking lot. Claire's car was already parked, engine off. She was sitting there, her fingers tight around the wheel like she was trying to get herself under control.

Five minutes passed. Then another car pulled in. Daniel Craig.

He parked at the opposite end of the lot, but there was no hesitation when he got out. He strode straight toward Claire's car, looking around once before she stepped out to meet him.

And then, right there, in the middle of the lot, she walked into his arms. It wasn't casual. It wasn't a brief, platonic touch. This was an embrace. A lingering, familiar one.

I lifted my phone and snapped pictures. Claire pressed against him, head tucked near his shoulder. Daniel, his hands firm at her waist, leaned in like he belonged there.

A few murmured words. A glance toward the motel office. Then they pulled apart, Claire brushing a hand over her face before she turned toward the front office. Daniel followed, close enough that their arms almost touched.

I took another set of photos. Then I sat back and let out a slow breath. Now I had proof. The only question was what I was going to do with it. I sat in my car, phone in my lap, watching the motel entrance like I was waiting for divine intervention.

Claire and Daniel had disappeared inside, which meant I had some time to sit with the absolute mess of what I'd just witnessed. The vice principal and the golden boy business man, meeting in a motel parking lot, embracing before slipping into a room together.

This was big. And yet, something was still nagging at me. I stared at the phone screen, scrolling back through my notes. Something about the burner phone. The message.

Meet at the usual spot. 8PM.

My stomach twisted. What if the meeting wasn't about Sandra? What if it wasn't some shady school board deal, or a criminal handoff, or whatever else I'd been picturing?

What if it was just... an affair?

Daniel Craig was married. Claire was single. If they were sneaking around, he wouldn't use his personal phone. Too risky. A burner made sense. And if he was careless enough to lose it—

Kade answered on the second ring. "Tell me you're not calling because you've done something reckless."

"That depends," I said. "Have you gotten the cell tower data yet?"

His silence told me everything.

"Not yet," he finally admitted. "Why?"

I exhaled, watching the motel doors. "Because I think I know whose burner phone it was."

Kade was quiet for a beat. "I'm listening."

I leaned back, playing with a loose strand of hair. "I just watched Daniel Craig and Claire Hanover meet at the Parkside Inn. Full embrace in the parking lot before heading into a room together. They're having an affair."

Another pause. Then, "Are you sure?"

"Pretty damn sure."

Kade muttered something under his breath, probably reworking every angle of the case in his head. "And you think the burner is connected to them?"

I nodded, even though he couldn't see me. "Think about it. A married man arranging a hookup with his mistress isn't going to use his regular phone. He's going to use something untraceable. And the message—'usual place. 8PM.' What if the usual place was the Parkside Inn? What if Claire and Daniel have been meeting there all along?"

Kade sighed. "That would explain a lot."

"It would," I agreed. "Like why Claire's been scrambling to cover her tracks."

"All right," he said. "I'll keep pushing for the cell tower records. But Audrey—"

"I know," I cut in. "Be careful."

"Yeah," he said. "That."

I hung up, staring at the motel across the street.

If Daniel had been using that burner phone to arrange meetups with Claire, what else had he used it for?

After an afternoon of obsessing, texting Kade for updates, and pacing my living room until I almost wore a groove in the floor, I finally accepted I wasn't getting answers while getting my steps in for the day.

I needed proof. Aside from Claire and Daniel's affair, that is. And for that, I needed Ben.

We crouched in the shadow of the school building, the glow from the streetlamp casting long shapes against the pavement. The whole place was locked up tight, but lucky for me, I had a built-in security bypass.

Ben walked through the back door, did a quick sweep, then popped his head through the solid wood with a dramatic flourish. "Your ghostly locksmith has arrived."

I crossed my arms. "Are you going to open the door or just show off?"

Ben grinned and stuck his hand straight into the key card reader. The little red light blinked green with a cheery beep.

I raised an eyebrow. "That's... disturbingly convenient."

"I know, right?" Ben waggled his fingers. "If I wasn't already dead, I'd have a career in high-end burglary."

I shoved the door open and slipped inside, heart pounding even though I knew no one was here. It wasn't *illegal* illegal if I was technically following a lead. Right?

We moved fast. Claire's office was exactly the way I'd left it earlier, pristine and controlled, everything in its place. Which was good for her, bad for her secrets. A person like Claire? She had things locked down. Except for the computer.

Ben hovered in front of it, his hands resting above the keyboard. The screen flickered, files shifting rapidly as he sifted through the digital wreckage Claire had tried to erase.

"I'm in her deleted folder now," he murmured.

I kept an ear on the hallway, my pulse steady but

ready to spike at the first sign of trouble. "Anything good?"

"You mean illegal, incriminating, or just plain shady?" Ben's lips quirked. "Because I've got all three."

I stepped closer as a list of recovered emails filled the screen. My gaze skimmed past the standard board correspondence until I landed on one that made my stomach tighten.

I know what you did.

I swallowed. "Open it."

Ben flicked his hand toward the screen, and the email expanded.

From: Sandra   Greaves (sgreaves@fireflybayes.edu)

To: Claire Hanover (chanover@fireflybayes.edu)

Subject: I know what you did.

The numbers don't lie.

That was it. No greeting. No further explanation. A chill worked its way down my spine. "Sandra knew," I murmured.

Ben exhaled slowly. "Looks that way."

My mind raced. Sandra had uncovered something before she died. She'd confronted Claire. And now she was dead. Was this what had gotten her killed?

I scanned the rest of the screen, heart thudding. "Is there anything else?"

Ben flicked through the recovered files. "Yeah. A forwarded financial report. Sent to Claire. The attachment's corrupt, but I can pull the metadata."

"Print whatever you can," I said, already moving to the corner of the room. I tapped the printer awake, and it hummed to life. The soft whirr filled the office as pages spit out one by one—the email from Sandra, the forwarded report, and a handful of other recovered messages.

And that was the moment the hallway lights flicked on. A voice echoed down the corridor.

"Hello?"

I froze.

Ben turned sharply. "That's not good."

Footsteps. Steady. Approaching.

I grabbed the last of the papers and smacked the cancel button on the printer. The machine choked mid-page, leaving a half-fed sheet hanging.

"Do something," I hissed.

Ben shot me an incredulous look. "Like what? Politely ask them to leave?" He pulled his hands from the computer, and the screen went black.

The doorknob rattled, and I nearly peed myself. I dove under Claire's desk, curling into a crouch as the office door creaked open. My breath caught in my throat. A pair of heavy work boots stopped inside the doorway.

Night security.

Ben hovered beside him, his face blank as he watched me panic from the safety of the incorporeal plane. The security officer sighed, muttering to himself, then stepped farther into the room.

I pressed myself tighter against the back of the desk, holding my breath, silently willing him to chalk up whatever he'd heard to the old building settling for the night.

The security officer grumbled something under his breath, moving toward the printer. The half-printed page was still sticking out. I swore internally.

Ben glanced at me. Then at the printer. Then back at me.

The security officer ripped the half-fed page from the machine and squinted at it.

Then he shook his head, sighed, and tossed it into the trash.

I stayed absolutely still as he walked to the door, flicked off the lights, and left.

The second his footsteps faded, I scooted out from under the desk, printed pages clutched to my chest, and shot Ben a glare.

He held up his hands. "What? Not my fault you panicked."

I exhaled sharply, swiping the half-printed page from the trash on my way out. Claire had deleted these emails for a reason. Sandra had uncovered something. And someone had made sure she never got the chance to talk about it.

***

I pushed through the front door, dropping my bag onto the entryway table with a satisfied sigh.

"I'm home, and I come bearing evidence."

The living room light was on, which meant Kade was still awake. And judging by the way he was standing in the kitchen, arms crossed, brows slightly raised, he wasn't exactly thrilled about my late-night escapades.

"You've been out skulking around in the dark again," he said.

I tossed my jacket over a chair. "Skulking is a strong word. I prefer 'investigating.'"

Kade didn't budge.

I sighed. "Okay, yes, I was skulking. But—" I brandished the printouts in the air. "Look what I found."

His gaze flicked to the papers. "Should I be impressed or deeply concerned?"

I grinned. "A little of both, probably."

Kade took the stack from me, flipping through the pages, his expression shifting from mild exasperation to full-on detective mode.

"Where did you get these?"

I pressed my lips together, then flashed him my most innocent smile. "It's best you don't ask."

He sighed. "Right. That's what I was afraid of."

"Listen, if it makes you feel better, I did not technically break any laws."

Kade shot me a dry look.

I raised my hands. "Okay, fine. Some laws may have been... gently nudged aside. But in my defense, I was very sneaky about it."

He rubbed his jaw. "And Ben helped."

"Oh, absolutely. He's very good at it."

As if summoned, Ben materialized in the middle of the room, arms crossed. "Did I just hear my name being used in vain?"

I gestured toward Kade. "He was questioning our methods."

Ben smirked. "Which ones? The morally gray ones or the highly illegal ones?"

Kade muttered something under his breath that sounded suspiciously like a plea for patience.

I plucked the papers from his hands, tapped the email from Sandra to Claire, and turned to Ben. "We need to talk to Sandra."

Ben mock-saluted. "On it, boss." He vanished, the air crackling faintly where he had been.

The room cooled slightly, that telltale ghostly chill sweeping through the space. A second later, Ben was back—and he wasn't alone. Sandra stood beside him, arms crossed, her gaze scanning the room as if she wasn't sure why she was here. A faint flicker of unease crossed her features before she masked it with a neutral expression.

She exhaled sharply. "This better be important."

I tilted the stack of papers toward her. "Oh, it is."

She hesitated before settling on the couch, her back straight, hands folded neatly in her lap. Despite the calm exterior, tension coiled beneath the surface, her fingers pressing into the fabric of her skirt.

She met my gaze. "Well?"

I studied her, noting the shift in her energy—less restless, but more wary. Something about this was already setting her on edge. I held out the printout of her email. "Did you send this?"

Sandra looked at the page, scanning it with a small frown. Her lips parted slightly, as if the words didn't quite make sense. Then she shook her head.

"No," she said quietly.

I blinked. "No?"

She looked at me then, confusion flickering across her face. "I... I didn't send this."

Kade raised an eyebrow from the kitchen. "You're interrogating an empty couch again."

I ignored him. "Are you sure?"

Sandra's grip on her skirt tightened slightly. "Yes. I may not remember dying, but I remember my life. And I would never send something like this."

I hesitated. "It came from your email."

Sandra's brows pinched together. "Then someone else sent it."

From the kitchen, Kade sighed loudly. "Let me guess. She's denying everything?"

I shot him a quick glare before turning back to Sandra. "You never typed this? Never even drafted it?"

Sandra pressed her fingers to her temple, thinking hard. Then she exhaled slowly.

"No," she repeated, but this time it sounded more bewildered than certain.

Kade muttered, "Ghost amnesia. Fantastic."

I ignored him again. "Sandra, do you have any idea what Claire was involved in?"

Sandra shook her head again. "No. I was always on the outside of things like that."

I hesitated, then decided there was no point in sugarcoating it. "She was having an affair."

Sandra blinked. "With who?"

"Daniel Craig."

Her lips parted slightly in surprise. "Is that right?"

I nodded.

She let out a slow breath. "That does explain a few things."

I leaned forward. "Like what?"

Kade groaned. "Could you please repeat what she's saying instead of just looking dramatic?"

I held up a finger in his direction but stayed focused on Sandra. "Like what?"

Sandra hesitated, as if sorting through her memories. "I always thought it was odd how much influence Daniel had at the school," she said slowly. "His sons, Ethan and Joshua Craig? Their paths were always smoothed over. Any issue, any hiccup—poof, gone."

I nodded. "Because of Daniel?"

Sandra frowned. "And Claire. They were close

when it came to the board. He pushed, and she made it happen."

Kade crossed his arms. "What are you agreeing with?"

I turned to him. "Sandra says Daniel had a lot of pull at the school, and Claire smoothed the way for him."

Kade nodded. "And yet Olivia Carter's kid got expelled."

Sandra's lips pressed together. "Exactly. That never sat right with me."

I repeated that to Kade, who muttered, "Now we're getting somewhere."

Ben, meanwhile, was smirking. "You should let him suffer a little longer. Maybe pretend I'm saying really alarming things."

Sandra, oblivious to the banter, rubbed her arms as if suddenly cold. "I don't like this," she admitted. "I feel like I should remember something about all this. But I don't."

I stood, shaking out the pages in my hands. This email changed everything. If Sandra hadn't sent it... who had?

CHAPTER SEVENTEEN

*M*orning came with a vengeance. My alarm blared, and I slapped at my nightstand in search of my phone. Missed. Instead of hitting snooze, I sent the damn thing flying off the edge of the bed. It smacked the floor with an unforgiving thud, and Thor, who had been curled up at the foot of the bed, let out an indignant yowl.

"Not my fault," I muttered, fishing around for my phone. By the time I found it—screen intact, miraculously—I was already awake enough to be annoyed about it.

I dragged myself out of bed, shuffling toward the kitchen where Kade had left coffee on the counter. *Bless that man.* Thor was parked next to his food bowl, glaring at it like it personally offended him.

Bandit, true to form, was halfway inside the pantry—which I was sure I'd locked before going to bed last night. I froze, coffee mug halfway to my mouth. "How—"

Bandit looked up mid-mission, an entire sleeve of crackers clutched in her tiny, guilty hands.

I narrowed my eyes. "Did you pick the lock?"

She blinked at me.

I pointed. "Did you steal my keys?"

More blinking.

Then she stuffed a cracker in her mouth and bolted for the hallway. Thor flicked his tail. "Maybe if you fed her properly, she wouldn't be forced into a life of crime."

I exhaled sharply, setting my coffee down just as my phone rang.

Kade.

Snatching up the phone, I glared after Bandit's retreating butt and answered. "Tell me you have something good."

"Depends," he said. "Do you want the good news or the news that makes me regret not chaining you to the couch?"

I frowned. "I feel like you just implied I need supervision."

"No 'imply' about it," he muttered. "I got a hit on your guy."

My breath caught. "The alley guy?"

"The very one."

I snatched my notebook off the counter, flipping to the section labeled *Sketchy Bastards*. "Who is he?"

"Name's Lyle Barker. Forty-four. Career criminal. Mostly intimidation, financial fraud, and breaking into places he shouldn't be."

I frowned, tapping my pen against the notepad. "You think he's the guy who broke into Priscilla's house?"

Kade hesitated. "Wouldn't be surprising. The guy's got a history of 'retrieval jobs'—as in, breaking in and taking things for people who don't want to get their hands dirty."

I paced to the window, staring out at the back garden and woods next door. If Barker had broken into Priscilla's house, then whoever hired him was looking for more than just that folder. What if they thought she had copies of the financial records? What if she did?

And if she had them, she might still be a target. I tightened my grip on the phone. "I need to talk to Priscilla again."

Kade groaned. "Of course you do."

"She could be in danger," I said. "And if she knows who's behind this, we need to find out."

"Fine," Kade said. "But be careful, all right?"

"My middle name is careful," I reassured him.

"Ha!" He barked out a laugh. "Your middle name is—"

I cut him off, "Gotta run. Love you. Bye!"

Priscilla wasn't going to like seeing me again. That was too bad. I pulled up outside her house and eyed the front door, debating whether to knock or just wait her out. I'd already spoken to her at the station after the break-in, and she hadn't exactly been forthcoming.

But now? Now I had a name. A reason to push harder. I climbed out of the car and headed for the door, knocking firmly.

Nothing. I waited a beat, then knocked again. Still nothing. I frowned, glancing around the front yard. Her car was in the driveway.

"She's home," Ben said, poking his head through the wall. "She just doesn't want to talk to you."

"You didn't have to come, you know," I grumbled,

only slightly disturbed at the sight of my best friend sticking his head through a wall.

"Does Kade know you're here?"

I sighed. "Yes, and don't start. He already gave me the *be careful* speech."

Ben lifted an eyebrow. "And yet, here you are. Alone. At a suspect's house."

"I'm not alone. I'm with you."

He grinned. "Good answer."

I knocked a third time. Louder. A shuffle of movement. Then a pause. Finally, the door cracked open, just enough for Priscilla to peek out. Her eyes were red-rimmed, like she hadn't slept much.

"What do you want?" Her voice was raw, tired.

"Can I come in?" I asked.

"No."

I sighed, leaning against the doorframe. "I'm not here to hassle you, Priscilla. I just need to talk."

She hesitated. "About what?"

"Lyle Barker."

The blood drained from her face. She didn't even try to hide it.

"I—I don't know who that is," she said too quickly. *Liar.*

I crossed my arms. "Funny, because he seemed to

know you. And I'm guessing that meeting you had with him in the alley wasn't for a friendly chat."

Priscilla shifted uncomfortably. "I already told you. I gave him the folder. That's all."

I leveled a look at her. "So, if I asked you whether he's the one who broke into your house, what would you say?"

Her fingers tightened around the edge of the door.

"Because I'm guessing he didn't find whatever he was looking for," I continued, watching her reaction. "And if he's still looking, that means you still have it."

Her breath hitched.

I dropped my voice. "Priscilla. If you have copies of those records, you need to tell me."

Her eyes darted past me, scanning the street, like she expected someone to be watching. "I don't—" she started, then stopped herself.

I waited. For a long second, she looked like she was about to slam the door in my face. Then, slowly, she exhaled. "Not here."

I lifted an eyebrow. "Where, then?"

She glanced over her shoulder, uneasy. Then she stepped back and opened the door.

"Come inside."

I stepped over the threshold, following her to the

kitchen where she stood, arms wrapped around herself, looking everywhere but at me. Her nerves were ramped up to eleven, and the longer she hesitated, the more convinced I was that I'd hit something big.

I leaned against the counter, keeping my voice even. "Tell me what you still have."

Priscilla's grip tightened on the back of a chair. "I don't have any copies of the reports."

I leaned back, eyes narrowing. "Then why is Lyle Barker so interested in you?"

She flinched.

Ben made a clicking noise with his tongue. "She knows exactly why."

I crossed my arms. "You didn't hand over everything, did you?"

She let out a slow, shaky breath. "I gave him the folder."

I stared at her. "And?"

Priscilla hesitated. Then, so quietly I almost didn't catch it: "...I took photos."

Ben perked up. "Oh, she's sneaky."

I exhaled. "Where are they?"

She hesitated again.

I pushed off the counter. "If you deleted them, I swear to—"

"They're on my phone."

Ben grinned. "Oh, now this I can work with."

I held out my hand.

Priscilla clutched the phone to her chest. "I need leverage," she whispered.

I studied her for a second. "Leverage against who?"

She still wouldn't look at me.

I sighed. "Priscilla, we are way past games. If you think Claire is coming after you, we need to know what's on those reports."

She licked her lips. Then, with extreme reluctance, she unlocked her phone and handed it over.

Ben cracked his knuckles. "Let's see what she's been hiding."

He placed his hand over the screen, concentrating as the data flickered beneath his touch.

"They're here," he murmured, unseen by anyone but me. "Yeah, same financial reports from Claire's computer."

I nodded, as if I had just found them myself. "Huh. Just as I thought."

Priscilla's expression stayed carefully blank. Ben

kept scrolling, faster now. His gaze snapped to something.

"Ohhh," he muttered. "Bingo." He pointed at the screen. "She's been texting Daniel Craig."

I blinked at the phone, scanning the screen. The messages weren't business-like. They weren't casual. They were—intimate.

I frowned, scrolling down.

Ben leaned in. "She was losing her damn mind over him."

I skimmed through the messages. Then I stopped. The words on the screen sent a sharp jolt through my chest.

Priscilla: You think I'm stupid? You told me I was the only one. Was that a lie, too?

Daniel: Babe, don't start this again.

Priscilla: I know about Claire.

Daniel: You're overreacting. It's not what you think.

Priscilla: Then tell me what it is.

Daniel: You're the only one I care about. You know that.

Priscilla: You didn't answer my call
last night. Were you with her?

Daniel: I was working.

Priscilla: Bullshit.

Daniel: You need to calm down.

Priscilla: You need to stop lying
to me.

This wasn't just an affair. Priscilla had been in love with him. And Daniel had been feeding her just enough sweet talk to keep her hooked. A fresh message caught my eye.

Priscilla: I bet you were with her last
night. That why you didn't answer?

Daniel: This is exactly why I didn't
answer.

My stomach twisted as I kept reading.

Priscilla: I saw how she looks at
you. How you look at her.

Daniel: We'll talk later. Stop texting
me on this number.

Priscilla snatched the phone out of my hands. "What the hell?" she snapped, clutching it to her chest. "You were supposed to be looking at the photos!"

I blinked at her, slow and measured. "I was."

Her nostrils flared. "Stay out of my business."

I crossed my arms. "You made it my business the second you got tangled up in this mess."

Her breathing was sharp and uneven. "Get out."

My stomach twisted. "Priscilla—"

"Now!" The fire in her voice left no room for argument.

Ben let out a long sigh. "That went well."

I shot him a look and turned toward the door. Priscilla didn't move, didn't breathe, until I was on the other side of it.

As the door slammed behind me, I let out a slow breath and tried to process everything I'd just learned.

Priscilla was in love with Daniel Craig.

Daniel was gaslighting her.

And now, I knew for a fact that her little trip to Claire's office wasn't about financial reports at all. She'd been looking for proof. Leverage to get Claire out of Daniel's life.

I sat in my car, gripping the steering wheel, waiting for my brain to catch up.

Priscilla. Daniel. Claire.

The web of lies, affairs, and manipulation was getting thicker by the second. And now, thanks to Priscilla's conveniently self-serving paranoia, I knew she wasn't some whistleblower seeking justice.

She'd been trying to get rid of Claire. And in the process, she'd stumbled into something bigger than herself.

Ben popped into the passenger seat, stretching his legs and crossing them at the ankles. "Well, that was a disaster."

I pinched the bridge of my nose. "Not entirely."

"Not entirely?" He scoffed. "You just got yourself kicked out of a suspect's house."

I shrugged. "Yeah. But I also got confirmation she was after Claire, not just dirt on the school board. And now we know she was in love with Daniel, was having an affair with him. And she knew about his affair with Claire."

Ben nodded, considering. "Okay. But are we just going to ignore the real problem here?"

I glanced at him. "Which is?"

"The fact that we still don't know what Lyle Barker actually wanted from her."

My stomach tightened. He was right.

Priscilla took those photos as insurance, but she hadn't exactly been careful about it. If Lyle had broken into her house searching for something, it meant he still hadn't found it. And if he hadn't found it, that meant he was still looking. Which meant Priscilla was still in danger.

I exhaled sharply and started the car.

"Where to?" Ben asked, watching me closely.

I hesitated. Then, with a slow breath—"I think it's time we had a chat with Daniel Craig."

***

The receptionist's polished smile faltered the moment I approached the desk. I didn't blame her— I didn't look like Daniel Craig's usual visitor.

"Mr. Craig doesn't take walk-ins," she said, polite but firm.

"Yeah, well, he'll make an exception." I flashed a smile. "Tell him Audrey Fitzgerald, private investigator, is here to see him."

Her hesitation told me she knew the name. Good. I folded my arms and waited. She picked up the phone. A clipped conversation later, I was escorted to his office with Ben trailing behind.

Daniel Craig's world was all glass, leather, and cold perfection. His office had the best view of Firefly Bay, and he sat behind a sleek desk, scrolling through something on his phone, completely unfazed by my presence.

"Miss Fitzgerald." He barely looked up. "I hope you didn't bully my receptionist too much."

Ben snorted. "Look at this guy. He *opens* with passive aggression. What a douche."

I dropped into the chair across from him, making myself comfortable. "Only a little."

He smirked—*calculated, measured.* "I'd ask what I can do for you, but I assume you're here to waste my time."

Ben paced behind me. "Classic narcissistic move," he grumbled. "Establish dominance. Undermine credibility. Do continue."

I mirrored Daniel's smirk. "You're sharp. Must be how you've kept your affairs so discreet."

The flicker was there—a half-second delay before he responded.

"Ooooh, did you see that? That was a micro-expression. He felt that one," Ben crowed.

Daniel exhaled a quiet laugh, finally setting his phone down. "Ah. You're here to talk about my personal life. That's... adorable."

I leaned forward. "Actually, I'm here about your *generosity.*"

That flicker again—barely there, but I caught it.

"Generosity?" he repeated, amused.

"You're a big donor to Firefly Bay School For Young Scholars. A real pillar of the community." I said. "How much have you funneled into that place over the last few years? Hundreds of thousands? More?"

His expression didn't change, but something shifted behind his eyes. "Private schools rely on support from families like ours."

"And that support comes with perks, doesn't it?" I leaned back. "Like making sure the right students stay enrolled, and the inconvenient ones get shown the door."

He chuckled, shaking his head. "I think you overestimate my influence."

Ben barked out a humorless laugh. "Oh yeah, buddy, we *really* don't."

"Do I?" I raised an eyebrow. "You and I both know Ethan shouldn't have coasted through this easily. His progress reports were underwhelming, his behavior was disruptive, and yet — no consequences, no intervention. Just smooth sailing, year after year."

His smirk didn't waver. "Are you suggesting I *bought* my son's education?"

"I don't know, Daniel." I shrugged. "Did you?"

Silence. Perfectly measured, perfectly timed silence.

Then he let out a quiet laugh. "You're amusing, I'll give you that. But this little theory of yours?" He shook his head. "There's no crime in giving back to the community."

"No, but there's *definitely* a crime in bribing a school official to keep your son enrolled." I let my words hang in the air.

Daniel didn't flinch. Didn't react at all. But I could feel it—the *shift*. Still, he played his part perfectly. "Miss Fitzgerald," he said smoothly, "I know you fancy yourself an investigator, but throwing random words together and hoping they stick isn't how this works."

Ben mock gasped. "Gaslighting, ladies and gentlemen! Give him a round of applause!"

I didn't blink. "I notice you didn't deny any of that."

His smirk widened. "You remind me of my wife. Always jumping to conclusions. Always convinced I'm hiding something." He tilted his head. "Samantha didn't send you here, did she?"

"Check out the blame shift. *She* is the problem, not *me*." Ben crossed his arms, a smug expression on his face, as if pleased he was accurately reading Daniel's behavior.

I shook my head. "Nope. I came on my own."

"Of course you did." He sighed, like I was a tiresome child. "People like you—you think you can walk in here, throw accusations at me, and what? I'll fall to my knees and confess?"

"That'd be convenient."

He laughed—actually laughed. "Let me give you some free advice," he said, leaning forward like he was doing me a favor. "If you want to be taken seriously, stop chasing conspiracy theories. You're embarrassing yourself."

"Aaaaand there it is." Ben fist pumped the air. "Undermining credibility. Ladies, gentlemen, ghosts —it's been a masterclass in manipulation."

I held Daniel's gaze, forcing myself to stay calm. "That burner phone," I said. "The one used to threaten me? It was connected to you. Maybe not directly, but close enough that Detective Galloway is already on it."

Nothing. No flicker of concern. Just that same practiced smirk.

"If that were true," he said smoothly, "I'd already be in handcuffs."

"And yet, here you are."

He opened his hands. "Here I am."

The silence stretched, thick and calculated. He was waiting for me to doubt myself. Waiting for me to make a mistake. I exhaled through my nose, rolling my shoulders back. "You know what I think, Daniel?"

He gestured for me to continue. Indulging me.

"I think you're very, very good at staying on the right side of trouble. I think you pick your words carefully, make sure everything is *just* deniable enough." I leaned in, lowering my voice. "And I think that's going to stop working very, very soon."

For the first time, his expression cooled. Not anger. Not panic. Just mild irritation, like I was a fly buzzing too close to his ear. Then he sat back, letting the moment pass. "Are we finished here?"

I smiled. "For now."

Ben moved to my side as I stood, arms folded. "He's good," he muttered.

"He's slippery," I muttered back. "But everyone slips up, eventually."

I walked out without another word, but I felt him watching me as I left.

CHAPTER EIGHTEEN

I stalked out of Daniel Craig's office, my jaw tight, my mind spinning. Behind me, Ben kept pace, hands shoved into his pockets. "Well," he said, glancing back toward the door. "That was fun. Let's never do it again. What a piece of work he is."

I yanked open the car door and slid inside, gripping the wheel a little tighter than necessary. "He's definitely involved. But deflecting."

Ben snorted. "Yeah, no kidding. That man gaslights so hard, I think he could power a city block."

I exhaled, forcing myself to loosen my grip. "Did you hear what he said about Samantha?"

Ben flopped back against the passenger seat.

"Which part? The casual sexism or the bit where he made her sound like a paranoid lunatic?"

"That one. He didn't even hesitate. Just—*snap*—Samantha jumps to conclusions. Like it's a script he's rehearsed a hundred times."

I turned the key in the ignition. Ben raised an eyebrow. "Where are we going?"

"To talk to the woman who's apparently been 'jumping to conclusions' her entire marriage." I shifted into drive, then added, "But if I'm going to interview another Craig today, I need caffeine first."

A few minutes later, I pulled into the coffee shop drive-thru, fully intending to enjoy a peaceful caffeine boost before heading to my next interrogation. What I hadn't intended? Scalding hot coffee cascading down my front the moment I took the first sip. I let out a strangled noise, jerking the cup away as it sloshed onto my shirt, my jeans, and quite possibly my soul. "Oh, come on!" I fumbled for napkins, but the damage was done. The brown stain spread across my chest.

Ben laughed from the passenger seat, taking one look at my disaster and shaking his head. "That's impressive. Really. I don't know how you manage to function daily."

"Shut up," I muttered, patting at the stain uselessly. "We have a job to do."

Ben smirked. "Right. Because nothing says 'professional investigator' like a woman who looks like she lost a fight with a latte."

Still scowling, I pulled up outside the Craig residence, tugging the edges of my jacket together in hopes of hiding the stain. It did not.

"So, what's the angle here? Because last time I checked, scorned wives weren't usually fountains of useful information."

"Daniel Craig is up to his neck in sordid affairs and lies, and I want to know if his wife has any idea," I muttered, swiping at the stain in a pointless attempt to salvage my dignity. "And Sandra was Ethan's teacher. I'm using that as an in."

Ben hummed. "And what exactly is the game plan? You gonna waltz in there and break the news that her husband's been giving out free trial runs to every woman in Firefly Bay?"

"No. That's a quick way to get thrown out," I said, unbuckling my seatbelt. "I'm here to ask questions about Sandra. Samantha doesn't need to know the rest."

"Mmm." Ben didn't sound convinced, but he gestured for me to get on with it. "I'll be doing some snooping while you make polite conversation. See if lover boy has a second burner phone lying around."

I sighed and headed up the driveway, knocking briskly on the door. A few moments later, the door swung open to reveal Samantha Craig. And just like her public image suggested, she looked like the perfect businessman's wife—polished, put together, not a hair out of place. The kind of woman who could host a fundraiser, bake cookies for the PTA, and politely ruin your career in the same afternoon.

Her smile was warm, her eyes bright with interest. "Oh, hello! Can I help you?"

I returned her smile with my best professional face. "Hi, Mrs. Craig. I'm Audrey Fitzgerald. I'm a private investigator looking into Sandra Greaves' death. I know this is short notice, but I'm speaking with some of Sandra's students' parents, trying to get a sense of how she was with the kids."

Her expression softened immediately. "Oh, of course. What an awful tragedy. Ethan adored Miss Greaves. Please, come in."

She stepped aside, and I walked into a house so pristine it made me instantly self-conscious. The scent of fresh flowers and expensive candles lingered in the air, and framed family photos lined the walls —images of a perfect family, smiling and happy.

Samantha led me into the kitchen, already moving to pour coffee. "Would you like a cup?"

I hesitated, then shook my head. "I just had one on the way over. Or... I did before I wore half of it."

She turned, eyebrows rising as she took in the coffee stain splashed across my shirt.

"Oh, dear. One second, I have something for that."

I expected her to grab a stain remover. Possibly a damp cloth. But instead, she disappeared into another room and returned holding a scarf. A really nice one. Possibly silk. Before I could utter a word of protest, she gracefully draped it around my neck, her fingers deftly adjusting the ends until the stain was artfully concealed beneath the folds of the exquisite fabric.

"Scarves are so multifunctional, aren't they?" she mused, stepping back to admire her handiwork. "Such a useful accessory."

I blinked, thrown by the unexpected gesture. "I —you don't have to—"

She waved off my protest with a conspiratorial smile. "Oh, please. It's synthetic, not silk. But don't tell anyone."

I let out a small laugh, almost afraid to touch the

silky fabric. "That's incredibly kind of you. Thank you."

"Of course! Now, sit, sit. Let's talk about Sandra."

"So Ethan really liked Miss Greaves?" I asked, keeping my tone light. "That's wonderful to hear. What was she like as a teacher?"

Samantha smiled fondly, wrapping her hands around her coffee mug. "Oh, she was wonderful. So patient. She really had a way with the kids, you know? Ethan adored her."

I nodded, scribbling a few meaningless notes. "Did Ethan ever mention anything about her? Any troubles she was having?"

Samantha hesitated, her brows knitting slightly. "No, nothing like that. If she was struggling with something, Ethan never mentioned it." She frowned. "Why?"

"Just covering all angles," I assured her, offering a small smile. "We're still piecing everything together."

Ben reappeared, leaning against the doorway, arms crossed. He shook his head—he hadn't found a burner phone.

Damn.

I refocused on Samantha. "I heard Ethan had a

fight at school last year," I said carefully. "Something with Elliot Carter?"

Samantha's brows lifted slightly, but she nodded. "Yes, that was an unfortunate situation. Boys being boys, you know. But it all worked out."

"I also heard Daniel met with Sandra about it."

Her expression softened. "Oh, yes. But not in the way people probably think. He wasn't upset with her at all. In fact, he was grateful. She was the one who convinced the school that Ethan shouldn't be expelled."

Ben and I exchanged an unseen glance. That was not the story Sandra had told me.

Samantha continued, unaware. "Daniel said Sandra saw the potential in Ethan and knew he wasn't a bad kid. She advocated for him. We were so grateful."

I nodded, keeping my expression neutral. "That must have been a relief."

"It was," Samantha agreed, smiling. "She was such a good person. She'll be sorely missed."

Ben let out a slow, silent whistle. Daniel Craig had fed his wife a completely different story. I reached into my bag and pulled out a business card, sliding it across the table. "If anything comes to mind, Mrs. Craig, please don't hesitate to reach out."

She took it with a warm smile. "Of course. I hope you find what you're looking for."

I thanked her for her time and stepped outside, Ben at my side. As soon as the door closed behind us, I exhaled.

"Well?" Ben asked.

I shook my head. "She doesn't know."

"Not a clue," he agreed. "She's got no idea who she's married to."

I sat in the car for a moment, drumming my fingers against the wheel as I processed everything. Samantha Craig had no idea. About Daniel. About his affairs. About the lies he spun so smoothly, she didn't even question them.

I let out a slow breath, my thoughts tangling together. This whole thing was getting messier by the minute, and I needed another perspective. Someone who could help sort through the threads before they knotted into an unsalvageable mess. Firing up the engine, I pointed the car toward the police station. If anyone could help untangle this, it was Kade. Besides, it was about time he got a full rundown on how deep this rabbit hole went.

"Now what? Dump everything on your husband and let him deal with it?" Ben asked from the passenger seat.

I chuckled. "Tempting, but no. I need to see what he makes of all this, though."

The drive was short, but my thoughts kept spinning, trying to piece everything together before reaching the station. By the time I pulled into the lot, I had more questions than answers.

Pushing open the door to the Firefly Bay PD, I strode inside, Ben floating beside me. Ignoring his usual commentary, I weaved through the bullpen toward Kade's office. His door was cracked open, but I knocked anyway because I wasn't a monster.

"Come in," Kade called, his voice distracted.

I stepped inside, Ben following close behind. Kade glanced up from behind his desk, eyes narrowing. "Tell me you haven't done something reckless."

"Ever notice how all your conversations start that way?" Ben said, perching on the corner of Kade's desk.

Ignoring him—again—I dropped into my usual seat and tossed my bag onto his desk, right through Ben's lap. "Depends on your definition of reckless. I had a nice chat with Priscilla Hawthorne. And by nice, I mean she kicked me out of her house after admitting she took photos of the financial reports before handing them over."

Kade groaned, rubbing a hand down his face. "Of course you did."

"Also," I continued, leaning forward, "based on the way someone broke into her house looking for them, I'd say she's not the only one who thought they were important."

Kade's jaw tightened. "That's dangerous, Audrey. You can't keep walking into these situations alone."

I waved a hand. "I wasn't alone. Ben was with me."

"Ben doesn't count."

Ben scoffed. "Rude."

Kade gave me a pointed look, but before he could launch into a lecture about safety and common sense, I dropped the real bombshell. "Daniel wasn't just having an affair with Claire. He was also sleeping with Priscilla. Two mistresses, Kade. *Two*. Who knows if there are more? The guy's a serial cheater."

Kade leaned back in his chair, letting out a slow breath. "Please tell me you didn't go running to Samantha Craig with that information."

I placed a hand on my chest, mock-offended. "Do you think so little of me? I didn't tell her. But I wanted to. Because, you know, the sisterhood—and because if you ever so much as contemplated stepping out on me, you'd be missing an important body part."

Kade smirked. "Duly noted."

I crossed my legs, shifting the scarf around my neck. Kade's eyes flicked to it, and he reached out, wrapping the fabric around his fingers before giving it a slight tug, pulling me closer. "New look?"

I snorted. "Funny story. Samantha gave it to me to cover up the coffee I spilled all over myself before I got to her house."

He hummed, running the silky fabric through his fingers. "You're going to shut this in a car door and accidentally strangle yourself, aren't you?"

I laughed. "Statistically? Probably."

His teasing faded into something more thoughtful. "You really think she doesn't know?"

"She's living in a bubble. She believes every lie Daniel feeds her." I exhaled, shaking my head. "She even thinks Sandra was the one who convinced the school to overturn Ethan's suspension. Kade, Daniel straight-up rewrote history for her, and she bought it."

Kade sighed, releasing the scarf and leaning back. "All right. We need to nail down who Lyle Barker is working for. If it's Daniel, we need hard proof. I'll push for any records we can pull on him—

phone logs, financials, anything that ties him to Craig."

I hesitated for half a second before adding, "I paid Daniel a visit."

Kade closed his eyes, exhaled through his nose, and muttered, "Of course you did."

I braced for it—the sigh, the resigned acceptance of my life choices—and sure enough, there it was. He ran a hand over his face before leveling me with a look that was equal parts exasperation and worry.

"Audrey," he said, his voice edged with something close to pleading, "you've already been threatened once."

"I know."

"And that doesn't make you want to, I don't know, *not* poke the guy who ordered it?"

I leaned against the desk, crossing my arms. "Poking him was the whole point."

Kade shook his head, rubbing the bridge of his nose. "One day," he said, "you're going to think twice before charging straight into the fire."

"I do think twice." I gestured vaguely. "Usually on the way in."

His jaw ticked, but he didn't take the bait. "What did he say?"

I straightened. "Exactly what you'd expect—

polished, smug, and impossible to pin down. He denied everything without actually denying anything and flipped the conversation back on me." I shifted in my seat, eager to move on from Daniel, the-very-annoying Craig. "What about the cell tower data? Is that in yet?"

"Lemme check." Kade turned his attention to his computer, fingers flying, tongue touching his lip as he concentrated on the monitor. "Good news. It just arrived."

"I'm on it!" Ben said from behind my left shoulder, making me jump. What was worse was he then proceeded to walk right through me, sending an icy blast through every single one of my internal organs.

"Ben," I hissed, doubling over in my chair.

"Audrey?" Kade was half out of his chair, concerned, when I waved him back down.

"I'm okay. It's Ben. He walked through me—he knows I hate it when he touches me. But he got excited about the data—he's analyzing it for you now, by the way."

Ben's concentration deepened, his eyes glowing faintly as he absorbed the data faster than any living person ever could. I drummed my fingers against Kade's desk, waiting.

Kade exhaled, running a hand through his hair. "If Ben can put the burner phone and Craig in the same location at the same time, we might finally have something solid."

I stifled a yawn, realizing how long this day had been, and it wasn't even lunchtime yet. A hot shower and a shirt that wasn't damp sounded more and more appealing. "All right, I'll leave you boys to it. I need to go home and change anyway—soggy coffee T-shirt is not a good feeling."

Kade exhaled through his nose, giving me a long, measured look. "Just..."

"I know, I know." I waved a hand. "I'll be careful. Scout's honor."

Before he could argue, I leaned across the desk and kissed him—slow, deliberate, and just long enough to throw him off. When I pulled back, a flush of red crept up his neck, his mouth slightly parted like his brain had momentarily short-circuited.

Grinning, I tapped a finger against his chin. "I'll see you later, yeah?"

CHAPTER NINETEEN

*P*ulling into the driveway, I shut off the engine with a sigh. The morning weighed heavily on my mind, but right now, all I cared about was getting out of my soggy, coffee-stained shirt and not being interrogated by a talking raccoon about my snack stash.

Making my way upstairs, I peeled off my damp clothes and stepped into the shower. The hot water cascaded over my shoulders, massaging away the tension knotted in my muscles. Closing my eyes, I let the warmth seep into every pore and work its magic to melt away the day's stresses.

A sudden scratching at the glass door made me jump.

"Mom! Mom! Mom!"

I cracked one eye open. Bandit was pressed against the glass, her tiny paws leaving streaks on the fogged-up surface.

"Spa treatment!" she declared, her nose twitching eagerly.

I sighed, reaching for the handle. "Bandit, you always regret this."

The second the door opened, she barreled in, standing proudly under the spray.

For two whole seconds.

Then she shrieked, did a panicked circle, and bolted, her soaking wet body slipping and sliding across the bathroom tiles. She skidded through the open door, leaving a trail of water in her wake, her distressed chittering echoing down the stairs.

Thor, perched on the counter, let out a satisfied sigh. "That was everything I hoped it would be."

Turning off the water, I reached for a towel when I heard an unmistakable throat-clearing.

"Gah! DAMMIT, BEN!"

I flailed wildly, nearly slipping as I wrapped the towel around me, shooting daggers at the ghost lounging by the sink, looking smug as ever.

"Chill. I'm dead, not a peeping Tom. I didn't see anything."

I hurled my shampoo bottle at him, which

predictably passed through his head, and clattered to the floor. "Very mature," he said with a smirk.

"Boundaries!" I jabbed a finger at him. "We've had this talk!"

"I bring news."

"And you're going to bring it from literally anywhere else."

Ben sighed with Oscar-worthy drama, but turned and walked through the wall. By the time I got downstairs, my pulse had stopped trying to punch its way out of my throat. The initial fury had burned down to a slow simmer—still annoyed, but no longer at risk of launching another missile at Ben's head.

At least I looked like someone who had their life together. Jeans, boots, T-shirt and a jacket weren't exactly high fashion, but they were functional, and more importantly, they kept me from feeling as exposed as I had moments ago.

The kitchen was quiet except for the low hum of the fridge, the kind of silence that made it easy to pretend I was the only one here. Fine by me. Moving on autopilot, I set up the espresso machine and pressed the button, waiting for the familiar hiss of steam. Caffeine first, dealing with spectral idiots second.

Ben was lounging by the fridge, arms crossed, completely at ease. "You look grumpy."

I shot him a look as I reached for a mug. "You have a real gift for understatement." He smirked, but didn't push his luck. Probably for the best. I sighed and rubbed a hand over my face. "It's been a morning, and it's not even noon yet. You mentioned news?"

"I checked the cell tower data."

I paused, hand hovering over my coffee mug. "And?"

"The burner phone was at The Daily Roast when it got that message Friday morning."

I exhaled slowly. "So now we know where it was. Question is—who sent it?"

He shifted, looking mildly uncomfortable. "Still working on that. The number was masked. Whoever sent it was covering their tracks."

I narrowed my eyes. "But you *can* crack it, right? You just need more time?"

He sighed. "Maybe. It's buried under so much rerouting and anonymizing, it's like peeling an onion. But I'll keep digging."

I exhaled sharply. "So right now, all we've got is this — someone sent a message to the burner phone

Friday morning, and whoever had it was at The Daily Roast."

Ben nodded. "You got it. Which means if we can check the security footage, we might see who owns the burner phone."

I perked up. "That's an actual plan. Let's go check."

Ben grinned. "Wow. No unnecessary risks or morally questionable ideas? Who even are you?"

"Give me a minute. I'm sure I'll do something stupid soon." Before I could spiral down that thought process, my phone rang.

Kade.

I answered instantly. "Hey, babe."

His voice was calm, but there was something in it that made me sit up straighter. "Are you home?"

"Yeah. Freshly showered and ready to face the day—again. What do you have?"

"Sandra's autopsy report just came in. Time of death is estimated between 7 and 10 PM Friday night. Cause of death is ligature strangulation."

I tightened my grip on the phone. "That fits the timeline of the burner phone message."

"It does," Kade agreed. "Has Ben managed to do anything with the cell tower data? Our techs are on it, but it could take a while."

"He sure has." I shot Ben a wink, grinning when his chest puffed out. "He's put the burner phone at The Daily Roast when the message was received. We're heading there now to see if we can take a look at the CCTV footage."

"Good luck with that," Kade snorted.

"It doesn't hurt to ask," I said defensively. "Plus, if they say no, I'll throw it to you, and you can get a warrant and make it all official."

"And in the meantime, you'll have Ben do his thing," Kade surmised.

I grinned. "And in the meantime, I'll have Ben do his thing," I confirmed.

The Daily Roast was packed when I walked in, the scent of ground coffee beans and burned milk hitting me as soon as the door swung shut behind me. The air buzzed with conversation, a steady hum of caffeine-fueled energy. The line stretched almost to the entrance, and I sighed, resigning myself to the wait.

I stepped into place behind a man in a suit who was typing furiously on his phone with one hand while juggling a takeaway cup in the other. A pair of teenagers stood ahead of him, whispering and giggling behind their phones. A woman in yoga pants at the front of the line was ordering what sounded like the most complicated coffee known to man.

Ben leaned against the bakery display. "This is a great use of our time."

I ignored him, scanning the room. The café was busy but comfortable, the mid-morning rush keeping the baristas hustling behind the counter. A couple in the corner shared a newspaper, their conversation low, and murmured. A man in a baseball cap hunched over his laptop, his fingers flying over the keyboard. A mother wrangled two kids near the pastry case, their sticky fingers leaving smears against the glass.

When I finally reached the counter, I smiled at the young barista. "Hey, I'll take a large cappuccino, extra shot. And a muffin. Surprise me."

She barely glanced up, moving on autopilot. "Anything else?"

I hesitated. "Actually, quick question for you."

"If it's about oat milk, we're out."

"Tragic, but I'll live. I'm a private investigator, and I was wondering if I could take a look at the security footage from Friday morning."

That got her attention. She blinked, then frowned. "You're a what now?"

"Private investigator," I repeated, keeping my tone light. "I just need a quick peek at the footage from Friday morning."

She chewed her lip, clearly thrown off by the request. "Uh. I don't think I can do that. Like, legally."

Ben leaned against the counter, watching with amusement. "Called it."

I ignored him. "I get it. Totally fair. But maybe you could check with your manager?"

The barista hesitated, then leaned back toward the kitchen window. "Jared!"

A muffled voice responded. "What?"

"There's a..." She looked at me, clearly unsure how to phrase it. "A detective? I think? She wants to see the security footage."

There was a beat of silence, then a bearded man in his early thirties appeared, wiping his hands on a cloth. He gave me a slow, assessing look before sighing. "Yeah, that's gonna be a no. We don't release footage without a warrant."

Ben made a little *ta-da* motion. "What did I say?"

I sighed. "Could you maybe tell me who was here that morning?"

Jared gave me a flat look. "It's a coffee shop. A *popular* one. Lot of people were here."

"Right," I muttered. "And none of them stood out? Look, I know this sounds...bizarre, but this is important. I'm working a murder case."

"I mean, people don't usually announce themselves as potential murder suspects when they order their lattes," he deadpanned.

Ben snorted. "I like this guy."

Before I could push any further, my phone buzzed in my pocket. I pulled it out and glanced at the screen. A message from my own number? What the hell? Frowning, I tapped it open. It was a screenshot. Of Lyle Barker. Sitting at a corner table, looking at his phone. The timestamp? One second after the burner phone received the message.

My gaze flicked to Ben. The smug expression on his face told me everything I needed to know. While we'd been standing here waiting for Jared to cooperate, Ben had been busy. Without me even noticing, he'd reached his hand through the counter, found the CCTV setup, and yanked the footage we needed straight from the system. Then he sent it to me—from my own damn number because, apparently, ghost hacking came with a sense of humor.

Ben grinned. "You're welcome."

Jared, who had been watching me curiously, raised a brow. "You gonna order something or just stand there holding up the line?"

I held up my ticket. "Already did. But thanks for the chat."

My mind was racing as I moved toward the pickup counter. The burner phone belonged to Lyle Barker. Now, we just needed to know who sent the message. And why? And how was this all related to Sandra's murder? *Simple.*

"Speaking of Sandra"—I turned to Ben—"where is she?"

"Were we?" Ben replied, and I frowned.

"What?"

"Speaking of Sandra?"

"Oh. Right. No. We weren't speaking of Sandra, but I was thinking of her—"

"And I am many things, but a mind reader, I am not," Ben drawled, then waved a hand for me to continue. "You were saying?"

"Just that I haven't seen her in ages. Where is she? I thought she'd be hounding me to find out who killed her, but she's been... I don't want to say suspiciously silent. But, like... where is she?"

Ben shrugged. "No idea, but I can go find her if

you like?" He didn't give me time to reply, just vanished. And that's when I realized every eye in the café was on me. Talking into thin air. With a grin and a shrug, I held up my phone in one hand and tapped my ear with the other. "Bluetooth," I mouthed, breathing a sigh of relief when everyone went back about their business without noticing there was no earbud in my ear.

Back in the car, I carefully placed my coffee in the cup holder and unwrapped my muffin, determined to make it through one meal without wearing it. Letting the coffee cool for a moment, I took a careful bite, then risked a cautious sip as I dialed Kade.

He picked up on the second ring. "Tell me you're calling to say you're on your way home to take a nap."

I swallowed another bite of muffin. "Tempting, but no. I've got something. The burner phone—it belongs to Lyle Barker."

Silence. Then, "You're sure?"

"Got him on camera, sitting in the café, looking at his phone one second after the message was received. It's his. It has to be."

Kade blew out a breath. "Shit. That complicates things."

"Yeah, well, here's another thought for you—if Lyle owns the burner phone, maybe he's the one who made those threatening calls to Priscilla and me?"

Another silence. Longer this time. "Audrey," Kade started, his tone shifting, "you are not going anywhere near him."

I licked a stray crumb from my lip. "I mean, I kinda feel like I should track him down."

"Absolutely not."

I frowned. "Kade, I—"

"No," he cut me off, firm in a way he rarely was. "Audrey, Lyle Barker is a career criminal. Fraud, intimidation, break-ins—that's his thing. And guys like him? They usually stick to intimidation and fraud, but if the stakes are high enough, they can escalate. If he threatened you, it wasn't just to scare you—it was a warning. And if he killed Sandra, you showing up on his radar isn't just reckless—it's stupid."

I swallowed, feeling the weight of his words settle over me. Kade wasn't just being overprotective —he was genuinely worried, and that scared me more than anything.

"Promise me you won't go looking for him," he pressed.

I hesitated.

Ben materialized in the passenger seat. "She's totally gonna go looking for him."

I sighed. "Fine. I promise I won't *actively* seek him out."

Kade groaned. "That's not a promise. That's a loophole."

I exhaled, pressing my forehead against the steering wheel for a moment. "I get it, Kade. I do. And I'm not trying to be reckless. But if you get a warrant for the café's CCTV, that gives you cause to bring Lyle in for questioning. Let me observe. Not sit in—just observe."

Kade was quiet for a long moment before exhaling sharply. "Fine. But only observing, Audrey. You'll be in a different room, behind the glass. If he even glances toward the observation window, you're out. Understood?"

"Understood. Love you!"

"Love you too."

After hanging up, I turned to Ben. "Would it be bad if I sent you off to find Lyle?"

Ben grinned. "You're terrible. But yeah, I can do that. But Kade's right." He sobered. "Lyle is a dangerous dude. And if you're already on his radar, then you need to keep your distance. So, yeah, I can find him, I can follow him, I can get all up in his business. But I'm not going to tell you where he is. Not unless you're with Kade and you relay that information directly to him."

I nodded. "That's fair. It's best I don't know." I wasn't stupid. I'd heed both Kade and Ben's warnings. I was in no hurry to get in over my head with a hired thug, potentially a hired hit man. I glanced in the rearview mirror, checking the empty back seat. "No Sandra?"

"Right! Yeah, she's at the school. Sitting in on Seb's classes. You know"—he leaned in conspiratorially—"just between you and me, I think she has a little crush on our Sebastian."

I laughed. "Cute. But also pointless. Not only is *she* a ghost, but *he's* gay."

Ben smirked. "Yeah, but love makes people do stupid things. Even the dead ones."

CHAPTER TWENTY

Silence filled the cab as I adjusted my ponytail, tightening the elastic as if that might help rein in my thoughts. Fragments of the case clashed, trying to form a pattern I couldn't quite see. Lyle Barker owned the burner phone. Kade was getting a warrant for the café's CCTV, which would give him reason to bring Lyle in. I'd observe from the safety of another room. All good things. Sensible things.

So why did I feel like I was missing something obvious?

Ben, still lounging in the passenger seat like he had all the time in the world—because he did— watched me with an expression that was half amusement, half exasperation. "You're thinking too hard."

"It's a talent," I muttered, taking another sip of my coffee. "Something isn't adding up. If Lyle owns the burner phone, and that phone was used to threaten both me and Priscilla, then he's connected. But is he the killer?"

"Or just the hired muscle."

I drummed my thumb on the steering wheel, replaying everything we knew, sifting through conversations, leads, threats. Something was at the edge of my memory, nagging at me.

I slammed my hand down on the wheel.

"Holy shit."

Ben grinned. "I love when you do that."

I turned to him, heart hammering. "Daniel. The messages between him and Priscilla."

Ben frowned. "What about them?"

"He told her to stop texting him on *that* number." I reached for my coffee, hand shaking slightly. "Which means—"

Ben's brows shot up. "Which means he has another number. Another phone."

We stared at each other for half a second before I threw the car into gear. "We need to talk to Priscilla. Now."

Priscilla Hawthorne yanked open the door, already scowling. "Are you kidding me? Again?" She crossed her arms, exasperation rolling off her in waves. "This is officially harassment."

I arched a brow. "Then you should probably stop answering the door."

Ben guffawed, slapping his thigh.

Priscilla's eyes narrowed, her lips pressing into a thin line. Then, with a sharp huff, she moved to slam the door.

I stuck my foot in the way. "I just have one more question. Promise."

Ben snorted. "That is such a lie."

Priscilla narrowed her eyes. "I have nothing else to say to you."

"Oh, I think you do." I leaned against the doorframe, unfazed by her attempt to look intimidating. "You saw messages from Claire to Daniel. Were those texts on his regular phone... or another one?"

A flicker of hesitation crossed her face—so brief, I almost missed it.

"That's none of your business."

"I mean, it kind of is," I countered. "Since I'm investigating a murder."

Priscilla's grip tightened on the door. "You're out of line. My relationship with Daniel has nothing to do with Sandra's death."

Ben studied her closely. "Yeah, it does. And lucky for us, now that I know what I'm looking for..." He grinned. "I can find it."

I watched, my eyes practically on stalks as Ben put his hand through Priscilla's pants pocket, presumably to make contact with her phone and not to feel her up because that would be, ugh, gross.

Priscilla scowled, shifting uncomfortably. She had no idea what was happening, but something was making her uneasy. Probably an icy cold blast from the ghost with his hand in her pocket, I'd say.

"Are you sure?" I said sweetly. "It's possible Daniel Craig isn't the man you think he is. He's certainly not the great catch you think he is." I sniffed, examining my fingernails. "What were you expecting to happen, Priscilla? That he was going to leave his wife for you?"

Her nostrils flared. "He loved me!"

I barked out a laugh. "And Claire. And goodness knows how many others. Maybe even Sandra."

"Sandra?" Priscilla scoffed. "That mousy thing? No. He'd never go for her."

"There's a chance he did, though. Seems to me he wasn't exactly discerning with his choices."

Ben cracked up laughing. "Harsh, Fitz. Harsh."

A flash of doubt crossed Priscilla's face. "He wouldn't." But she didn't sound so sure.

"We both know he would," I lied. I mean, I had no idea if he'd tried to pursue an affair with Sandra or not, but the possibility was there. "And maybe you found out. And that's why you killed her."

Ben shot me a look. *Do you actually think she killed Sandra?*

Priscilla's face went pale, but she squared her shoulders. "I did not kill that woman."

"Then you won't mind telling me where you were on Friday between 7PM and 10PM."

Her jaw tightened. "At a gallery opening. There were at least thirty people there who can vouch for me."

Ben tilted his head. "Convenient."

Priscilla looked at me smugly. "Satisfied?"

"Not quite," I said.

Her expression faltered.

"Schools are busy places," I continued. "Students and teachers in and out of classrooms all day. You had access to Sandra's classroom. Her computer. You knew she often left it logged in."

Priscilla's fingers curled around the edge of the door. "So what?"

"So," I said, "that email Claire received from Sandra's account? The one Sandra didn't send..." I let the words hang between us, watching for a reaction. There it was—a tiny flicker of unease. I leaned in. "You sent it."

Priscilla scoffed. "That's ridiculous."

I crossed my arms. "Is it? You saw an opportunity and took it. You typed that message, fired it off, then deleted it from her sent folder so she'd never know."

Her lips pressed together.

I pressed on. "What was the goal, Priscilla? To rattle Claire? To make sure she knew someone was onto her without realizing it was *you*? Or were you just stirring the pot, hoping for a reaction?"

Her nostrils flared. "You can't prove that."

I huffed out a laugh. "Maybe not. But you haven't denied it either."

Priscilla glared at me. "Are we done here?"

I pushed off the doorframe, stepping back. "For now. But don't go too far. Something tells me we're gonna need another chat soon."

Priscilla slammed the door shut, and I turned to Ben. "Did you get it?"

"Got it. Daniel Craig's second number. Well, what I think is his second number. It was saved in her contacts under 'DC'. Real subtle."

I strode back to the car, my mind already sorting through what we'd learned. Ben materialized in the passenger seat as I slid behind the wheel, his expression thoughtful.

"Well?" he asked as I started the engine.

"She has an alibi," I admitted, starting the car. "One that we can check easily."

Ben hummed. "Doesn't mean she's clean."

I pulled out onto the road, my thoughts swirling. "No, it doesn't. The biggest link we have right now is Daniel's second phone."

Ben leaned back. "Agreed."

"What are the odds that he still has it?"

Ben shrugged. "Depends. If he thought it could get him in trouble, he might've ditched it. But if he's still using it…"

I nodded. "Then we need to track it."

Ben cracked his knuckles, which was entirely unnecessary, considering he had no bones. "Let me get on that." He vanished before I could respond.

Back home, I went straight to my office, where the whiteboard took up most of one wall. Names, notes, and connections sprawled across it in dry-erase marker—a chaotic snapshot of the storm in my brain.

I scanned the mess, searching for patterns, but nothing new jumped out at me. With a sigh, I dropped into my chair and fired up the computer, fingers flying over the keyboard as I updated my notes. I typed up everything we had so far—Lyle's connection to Daniel, the burner phones, Priscilla's alibi—trying to weave them into something that made sense.

A cold ripple ran through the air a second before Sandra materialized near the board, arms crossed, eyes narrowed. "You've been busy."

I barely looked up. "That's the job."

She hesitated, her gaze flickering toward the board. "Ben was watching me today. You sent him, didn't you?"

I sighed, finally turning to face her. "Yeah. I wanted to make sure you were okay."

Sandra frowned. "You're lying. You were checking if I remembered something."

I didn't deny it. "So? Do you?"

She shifted, her translucent form flickering. "No."

"Why hang out at the school then? Why abandon the investigation?"

Her hand went to her throat. "I haven't abandoned the investigation." She seemed truly affronted that I thought that. "I was just…" She waved a hand around, seemingly searching for the right words. "You have this all under control," she finally said. "And I missed… being alive, I guess? I missed work. And then I met Seb, and I figured I'd go see him, see how he teaches, and y'know, he hooked me right in." Her whole demeanor changed, and her face lit up. "He has such an engaging teaching style. The students love him, and I can see why. So, I stayed because… I enjoyed it."

I nodded. "Fair enough." I turned back to my computer, opening up social media. If Priscilla was telling the truth about her alibi, then there had to be proof. A gallery opening wasn't exactly a private affair—someone would have posted pictures, tagged friends, maybe even uploaded a video.

Sandra hovered over my shoulder, watching curiously. "What are you looking for?"

"Receipts," I muttered, clicking with the mouse. I navigated to the gallery's official page first, scrolling through event photos. Glossy, artsy shots of wine glasses, abstract paintings, and well-dressed patrons filled my screen.

Ben reappeared next to Sandra, peering at the screen. "Ooh, fancy. Think they'd let me haunt an art exhibit?"

"You can haunt whatever you want," I said absently, clicking through images. "Aha!"

I enlarged a group photo, and there she was—Priscilla, mid-laugh, standing next to a man in a navy suit, glass of champagne in hand. The timestamp put her at the gallery at 9:12 PM. Not airtight, but it was looking more and more like she was telling the truth. I exhaled. "Well, that's one alibi that checks out."

Ben nodded. "That means our list of suspects just got shorter."

Sandra drifted to the board again. "Then who's next?"

I turned in my chair to face Ben. "Tell me you found something."

He grinned. "Daniel's second phone is still active. And guess what? It just pinged off a tower near his office."

I sat up straighter. "He still has it?"

Sandra spun to face us. "Can you get into it? See the messages?"

Ben smirked. "Already did."

I blinked. "What?"

"Found the burner locked up in his desk at work," Ben said, stretching like he actually had muscles that needed loosening. "Phased right in, did a little tech magic—bam. Got the messages."

Sandra folded her arms. "And?"

Ben waggled his brows. "Well, surprise surprise, our boy Danny has been a busy little schemer. Messages between him and Lyle? Check. Claire? Check. Priscilla? Also check."

I leaned forward. "Anything new?"

Ben hesitated. "Nothing we didn't already suspect. But no mention of Sandra. At all."

That gave me pause. "Not even a hint?"

"Nope." Ben's face grew more serious. "But I did find confirmation that Daniel ordered Lyle to retrieve the folder of financial reports from Priscilla. By saving Claire, he was saving himself. He can't afford scrutiny on those transactions, so of course, he wanted that folder back."

I exhaled. "So, Daniel's hands aren't clean, but there's nothing tying him directly to Sandra's murder."

"There *is* something you might find interesting," Ben said, walking through my desk and laying a hand on my computer. The monitor flickered, static crackling for a second before my email inbox opened—except I hadn't touched the mouse. A new message sat at the top, sent from *my own damn email address*. I clicked it, and there they were. Messages between Daniel and Lyle.

> Daniel: You sure she didn't make copies?

> Lyle: Checked her place. Nothing on her laptop. Even swung by the school after hours Friday.

> Daniel: And? Anything?

> Lyle: Nothing. But she told you she took photos, right? That means they're on her phone.

> Daniel: Then get the damn phone. I don't care how. Just make sure she doesn't have anything left to send.

> Lyle: I'll take care of it. Got a plan in place.

Sandra stiffened beside me, her form flickering slightly. "Lyle was at the school that night?"

"Yeah," I confirmed, watching her closely. "Friday evening, after hours."

She pressed a hand to her temple, her brows knitting together. "I... I heard someone. I remember now. The door handle jiggled like someone was trying to get in. I thought it was a student messing around, so I went outside to tell them off. But it wasn't a student. It was him."

Ben straightened. "And? What did he say?"

Sandra hesitated, her fingers gliding over her throat. "He made up some excuse. Said he needed to grab a book for his kid's homework. I told him, 'It's too late.' That was the phrase, wasn't it? The one that witness overheard?" She looked at me. "That was me, talking to him."

A cold knot tightened in my stomach. "But you said you didn't recognize him before. You saw him in the alley with Priscilla. You saw the photo I took—"

Sandra shook her head. "It was dark. He kept his face in the shadows. I didn't get a clear look at him. But now, remembering the way he spoke, the way he moved... it was definitely him."

I exhaled slowly, frustration and relief mixing uneasily. Ghosts and their delayed memories. I got it, I really did—trauma messed with a brain, even a dead one—but damn if it didn't make my job harder.

Still, at least now we had an answer. The argument outside the school? Lyle and Sandra. His text proving he was there? Confirmed.

But did that mean Lyle was the killer?

Because as much as I turned it over in my mind, I still couldn't find the motive. Not for him. Not for Daniel. Not for anyone.

And that? That was a problem.

CHAPTER TWENTY-ONE

From behind the station's two-way mirror, I watched Kade work Lyle over in the interrogation room. The tension in there was thick enough to choke on, and if I were a better person, I might've felt sorry for Lyle Barker. But I wasn't, and I didn't.

I hadn't planned on spending my morning at Firefly Bay PD, but after piecing together the messages from Daniel's burner phone, it hadn't taken long to call Kade and fill him in. A warrant had gone out for Lyle's arrest within the hour, and Daniel Craig wasn't far behind.

Now, I just had to sit tight and hope Kade could squeeze something useful out of Lyle before Daniel found a way to slip through the cracks.

Lyle sat stiffly across from Kade, his arms crossed, jaw tight. He gave off the distinct air of a man who thought he was too smart to be sitting there—and also that he might throw a punch at any second.

Kade flipped through a file, casual as ever. "You've got quite the track record, Lyle. Fraud, intimidation, breaking and entering... You've been busy."

Lyle didn't blink. "You planning to charge me with bad life choices, or do you have an actual point?"

Kade smirked. "Oh, I've got a point." He slid a printout across the table. "You like making phone calls, Lyle?"

Lyle's expression didn't shift. "Depends."

Kade tapped the paper. "A call was made on this date, at this time, from a burner phone to Audrey Fitzgerald. Digitized voice. Ring any bells?"

Lyle didn't blink. "No idea what you're talking about."

Kade smirked, flipping to the next page. "See, that's interesting, because this particular burner phone was traced back to a purchase made with cash at a gas station. Security footage caught the buyer—you."

A muscle in Lyle's jaw twitched.

Kade sat back, letting the silence stretch. "Here's the deal, Barker. You're on the hook for a lot already. You threatened Audrey Fitzgerald. That's not up for debate. The only question left is—was that your idea? Or did Daniel Craig tell you to do it?"

Lyle exhaled sharply, shoulders tightening.

Kade pushed. "You think covering for him is going to get you out of this? Because let me tell you what he's saying about you." He slid another page across the table—Daniel's signed statement. "That call? That was *your* idea. According to him, he told you to 'handle it,' and you went straight to intimidation."

Lyle scoffed, but the slight flicker of unease didn't go unnoticed.

Kade's tone stayed level, steady. "You're looking at a lot of time, Lyle. But if you tell me exactly how deep Daniel's involvement goes, maybe we can talk about deals."

Lyle swallowed, staring at the papers in front of him. Then, finally, his shoulders sagged.

"He called me after Claire freaked out," he muttered. "Told me some PI had been sniffing around. Said he didn't need the extra heat."

Kade nodded. "And you figured a death threat would solve the problem."

Lyle's lips barely moved, his voice flat. "Usually does."

Kade didn't react, just flipped the page again. "And Sandra Greaves? What was that, Lyle? Just a scare tactic, too?"

Lyle's mouth pressed into a thin line.

"Here's the thing," Kade said, voice going dangerously soft. "We already know what Daniel told you to do. The only thing left is whether you want to go down protecting a man who's already selling you out."

Lyle's eyes flicked to the glass, as if calculating how much trouble he was really in. My spine stiffened, and I couldn't help the involuntary half step back. He couldn't see me, but for a second, it felt like he could—like he knew I was there, watching, waiting.

Which was ridiculous. And yet, my bladder suddenly had *thoughts* about the situation.

Kade leaned forward. "Tick-tock, Barker."

I crossed my arms, watching Lyle process just how screwed he really was. Then, for good measure, I crossed my ankles too—just in case.

He hadn't cracked—yet. But the shift in his posture, the way his fingers twitched against the table, told me Kade was getting to him. Daniel had thrown him to the wolves. That much was obvious. And now, Lyle had two choices: keep his mouth shut and take the fall or start talking and drag Daniel down with him.

I exhaled, my fingers drumming against my arm. *Come on, Barker. Spill.*

I pushed off the wall, glancing one last time through the one-way mirror. Lyle wasn't breaking yet, but the cracks were showing. Kade had him cornered—he just needed time to press harder.

I didn't have time.

"I'm going to see Claire," I muttered under my breath, already turning for the door.

Ben drifted through the wall and fell into step beside me. "Because that went so well last time?"

I rummaged in my bag for my keys, flashing the officer on duty at the front desk with a quick, innocent smile. "I need to push her."

Sandra materialized beside the station's exit, arms crossed tight over her chest. "You really think she had something to do with it?"

I hesitated, the cool metal of the door handle pressing into my palm. "I don't know yet," I admitted. "But I'm hoping being around her might shake something else loose."

Sandra didn't move. She was staring past me, her gaze locked on something only she could see. "I was so sure I'd never seen that man before," she murmured.

Ben and I exchanged a glance.

"But now you remember," I said.

She nodded, fingers tightening over her arms. "I remember the way he kept to the shadows, how he made sure I never got a good look at his face. How he told me he needed to grab something for his kid's homework. I didn't believe him, but it was late, and I was tired. I didn't press. I should have pressed."

My stomach twisted at the guilt in her voice. "Hey," I said gently. "This isn't on you."

Sandra swallowed, then lifted her chin. "Then let's go. Perhaps I'll remember more."

Ben let out an exaggerated sigh as he floated toward the door. "Great. Field trip with a traumatized ghost and a PI who never learned the definition of 'lie low.' Love this plan."

"You could stay here," I offered, pushing open the door and stepping into the cool afternoon air.

He scoffed. "And miss the fireworks? Absolutely not."

Sandra shot him a sharp look. "Yeah, 'cause this is *so fun* for me."

His smirk vanished instantly. "Okay. Fair point."

The school hallways were quieter than previous visits, the hum of midday classes leaving the corridors feeling eerily empty. I strode toward Claire Hanover's office with a sense of purpose, my footsteps loud on the linoleum floors. Ben and Sandra flanked me, neither speaking but both radiating anticipation.

"She's going to be thrilled to see you," Ben muttered.

"Mm-hmm," I said, unfazed.

Sandra was uncharacteristically quiet, her expression unreadable. Maybe she was still grappling with the memory that had surfaced earlier, or maybe she was tired of all the dead ends. Either way, I wasn't about to let Claire wriggle out of this conversation.

Reaching her office, I rapped on the door twice before turning the handle and stepping inside. Claire looked up from her desk, her expression shifting from polite curiosity to guarded suspicion. "Ms. Fitzgerald. This is a surprise."

"I was hoping to have a word."

Her fingers curled around the pen she'd been holding. "If this is about—"

I didn't let her finish. I kicked the door shut behind me and folded my arms. "Tell me, Ms. Hanover, what do you think the parents of this school would have to say about you sleeping with Daniel Craig? Not only a married man, but a benefactor of the school and parent to two of your students."

"Going in hot, eh, Fitz." Ben applauded, moving to the far wall to watch proceedings. Sandra hurried over to his side as if unsure what to do with herself.

Claire's breath hitched. Sweat beaded at her temple as she shot a glance behind me, like she was calculating her chances of making a run for it.

"What?" Her voice was hoarse, barely a whisper.

"You heard me," I said coolly, stepping closer. "I know you're sleeping with him—I saw you with my own two eyes. Lord only knows I wish I hadn't."

Claire opened her mouth, then shut it, her throat working as she struggled for something—anything —to say. She settled on the worst possible response. "It's not what you think."

I scoffed. "Oh, really? Because it sure looked like you were wrapped around him like a cheap scarf. Enlighten me—what exactly do I think is happening here?"

She sagged back in her chair, a tremor in her hands as she reached for the pen again, like it was some kind of anchor. "I love him."

I snorted. "That's adorable. Do you think he loves you? Because newsflash, sweetheart—he's been telling Priscilla the exact same thing."

Her eyes went wide. "What?"

"Oh, you didn't know?" I feigned shock, pressing a hand to my chest. "Claire, I'm so sorry to be the one to tell you, but Daniel's been spreading his affections around. Priscilla Hawthorne ring a bell? Or were you too busy being the other woman to notice there was yet another woman?"

Her entire body went stiff, her fingers tightening around the pen so hard I half-expected it to snap. "No. You're lying."

Ben, who had been leaning against the bookshelf, whistled low. "This is getting good."

"I don't lie, Claire," I said, my voice steady—an impressive feat, considering the blatant lie I'd just told. "And I've got the receipts. I've seen the texts, the sweet nothings, the promises. Just like he promised you, he promised her."

She looked away, her lips pressing into a thin line. "What do you want?"

"I want to know about the money," I said bluntly. "The donation Daniel made. The one you funneled to the Carters."

Claire flinched. "That was—it wasn't—"

"It wasn't what? Illegal? Because it sure as hell was unethical."

Her breath hitched. "I was trying to help."

"Help who? Olivia Carter? Or Daniel?"

Tears welled in her eyes, and she shook her head. "You don't understand. He *promised* me. He promised we'd be together. That I wouldn't have to hide anymore. That the school—" Her voice cracked. "I love him."

And just like that, the dam broke. Claire crumpled, sobs racking her frame. Her hands shook as she covered her face, shoulders trembling. It wasn't a few delicate tears—it was full-body, snot-filled devastation. A woman who had clung too tightly to a dream only to watch it crumble.

I should've felt smug. I should've felt righteous. But all I felt was tired.

Sandra's head jerked up, eyes wide. "That sound—"

Ben turned to her. "What sound? The howling banshee?"

"That cry. I *know* that cry." Her expression twisted in shock. "I heard it that night."

My stomach dropped, and I glanced at Ben, who looked as dumb-struck as I felt. "You're sure?" he asked.

Sandra nodded slowly, her brow furrowing. "I didn't recognize it then. I thought I was overhearing something real, like it was unfolding around me after I'd died. But it wasn't." Her voice wavered as realization set in. "It was a memory. And now I know —it was Claire."

I turned back to the woman still sobbing into her hands. She had no idea that, in this moment, her breakdown had just put her squarely at the center of Sandra's last known night alive. And suddenly, I had a hell of a lot more questions.

I folded my arms, watching Claire like a hawk. "See, I thought your affair with Daniel was your biggest secret. But then I remembered—you've got more to lose than just your reputation. You've been shifting school funds around like a damn magician."

Claire flinched like I'd struck her. "It—it wasn't

like that. Look, I love Daniel, I truly do, but his dedication to those brat kids of his? Off the charts. He donated to the school to sweep Ethan's latest discretion under the rug, and poor Elliot was *expelled*. Olivia was beside herself. So, I simply sent her the money. Said it was compensation from the school."

I leaned in. "The thing is, I'm not the only one who knows you funneled that money to the Carter family. Priscilla took copies of those records."

Claire's breath hitched. *This was new information to her.*

"She what?" Her voice cracked, eyes darting around the room as if expecting Priscilla to appear at any moment.

"She stole the file and took photos before Daniel sent his hired muscle to get them back." I tilted my head. "And that, Claire, is the real problem, isn't it? You could handle losing Daniel. But your job? Your career? That's something you'd do anything to protect."

Claire's eyes filled with panic. "No. No, that's not —" She shook her head as if trying to will the reality away. But it was too late. The damage was done. She knew what Daniel had done behind her back. That *Priscilla* had the power to destroy her.

"Let's get back to Friday night," I continued, while she was still off balance. "You were seen crying at the school. Why?"

Claire answered without hesitation, as if the words had been waiting to spill out. "I met Daniel in the parking lot. I told him I wanted to go public. That I was tired of the hiding. But he wouldn't hear of it. He said he was handling things, but if I kept up with the pressure, he'd break things off. *With me.* All this time, he'd been stringing me along, telling me he was going to leave his wife, when he..." She trailed off, mind reeling at the revelations I'd delivered.

"What happened after?"

She was shaking now, completely thrown. "I—I left. I went home."

I studied her, chin lifting. "You sure? Because something isn't lining up."

Claire pressed a trembling hand to her forehead. "I just—I sat in my car for a while, okay? I was upset. I didn't—"

I didn't buy it. "Did you hear something? See something?"

She shook her head, her face a mess of tear tracks and smeared mascara. "No. I swear, I—I didn't see anything."

I pressed. "You sat in your car. For how long?"

Claire sniffled, trying to pull herself together. "I don't know. Fifteen, twenty minutes? Long enough to calm down. I was upset. I—I thought maybe he'd come after me. Try to stop me from leaving." She let out a bitter laugh. "He didn't."

Ben scoffed. "Ouch."

I ignored him. "And then?"

"I was just about to start the car when I saw headlights."

A prickle ran up my spine. "Daniel's car?"

She nodded slowly, her hands twisting in her lap. "I thought maybe he changed his mind. That he was coming to find me. But then..." Her forehead creased. "He didn't park in the lot like before. He pulled around to the back entrance. And then—" She stopped, looking at me like she'd just walked herself into a trap.

I leaned in. "And then?"

Claire swallowed hard. "I left. I didn't see anything else. I didn't want to sit there waiting for him to come up with more excuses, so I just... I left."

I studied her carefully. If she was lying, she was damn good at it. But if she was telling the truth, then—

Sandra, who had been staring at Claire with a

strange intensity, suddenly inhaled sharply. "Oh, my god."

Ben and I both turned to her. "What?"

Sandra's expression twisted, her hands flying to her mouth. "The headlights. That car—" Her voice dropped to a whisper. "I saw it."

My breath caught. "Sandra, are you saying—?"

She nodded slowly. "I remember seeing that car the night I died."

Claire flinched. It was small—barely there—but I caught it. The slight jerk of her shoulders, the way her breath hitched, her fingers twitching at her sides like she wanted to grab onto something solid.

And that's when I realized—I'd said Sandra's name. Out loud. I barely had a second to panic before Claire's eyes snapped to mine, confusion warring with something else.

"You just—" She stopped, inhaled sharply, then shook her head. "What did you just say?"

Ben, standing off to the side, let out a low whistle. "Oh, this is gonna be good."

My mouth worked faster than my brain. "What?"

Claire gestured vaguely to the space between us. "You said Sandra."

Sandra tensed beside me, her expression unreadable. "That's unfortunate."

I swallowed. "Did I? No. No, I didn't."

Claire blinked. "You did. You literally said her name."

Ben grinned. "I mean, technically, you did."

I exhaled through my nose, offering Claire my most patient, vaguely amused smile. "I was talking about the case. It's been a long day, Claire." I sighed, rubbing my temple for good measure. "Probably just muttering to myself, working through everything."

Claire's brows pulled together. She wasn't convinced, but she wasn't completely sure either. "You weren't working through anything. You were talking. Like—" She shook her head again, pressing her fingers against her forehead like she could massage the moment out of existence. "God, I don't know. Maybe I misheard."

Ben leaned toward me. "Wow. I can't believe that worked."

"That seems likely," I said, as reassuring as I could manage. "You've had a hell of a day."

Claire let out a shuddering breath, rubbing her arms. "I—I need some fresh air."

Sandra nudged me. "Now's your chance. Get out before she starts thinking again."

I took a careful step back toward the door. "You should. Take a minute. Breathe."

Claire nodded absently, already turning away, her focus slipping in on itself. She wasn't entirely present anymore, and I wasn't about to stick around and let her brain catch up.

"I'll get out of your way," I said, reaching for the doorknob. Claire didn't even look up.

I stepped outside, pulled the door shut behind me, and exhaled.

Ben appeared beside me, arms crossed, smirking. "That was an Oscar-worthy performance."

Sandra snorted. "I thought she had you."

I shot them both a glare as I walked toward my car. "That was a close call." That was all I was willing to concede.

Ben shrugged. "You're slipping, Fitz."

Sandra smirked. "You do tend to talk to us a *lot*."

I groaned. "I hate you both."

CHAPTER TWENTY-TWO

By the time I got home—again—I was running on caffeine and stubbornness. It felt like I'd spent the entire day bouncing between locations, chasing leads, only to end up right back here, staring at the same whiteboard, searching for answers.

Ben stood beside me, arms crossed, nodding like he was deep in thought. For a moment, I assumed he was analyzing the case, sifting through the evidence the way a former detective should.

Then he said, "I wonder if a Samurai 3000 knife would cut tomatoes, or would you need the Samurai 5000 for that?"

I blinked. "What?"

Ben gestured vaguely at nothing. "Saw it on the

shopping channel earlier. They cut through a tin can like butter, but they never show them slicing a tomato, which is the real test."

Sandra groaned. "I died for this."

"We're missing something," I muttered, ignoring them both. "We've got all these puzzle pieces, but they don't fit the way they should."

I dropped into my chair, fingers drumming against the desk. "Ben, I need you to check the cell tower data again."

Ben shot me a look. "Did that twice already. What are we looking for?"

"I don't know yet," I admitted, pushing back the loose strands of hair that had escaped my ponytail. "Daniel's whereabouts, I suppose. He argued with Claire in the school parking lot. Then he left. Then she saw his car return. But the data puts his cell phone at home. With him. So, who the hell was driving?"

Ben straightened, interest piqued. "That's actually a solid question." He phased over to my computer, resting a hand on it. Static flickered, and the screen updated with a string of digital pings. "Okay, let's see. Daniel's phone connected to his home Wi-Fi at 8:47 PM."

I nodded. "Meaning he was home."

"And his phone never left," Ben confirmed. "And I'm pretty confident in saying there's no way he'd leave his phone behind. He wouldn't risk his wife seeing something she shouldn't."

"Right, so if Daniel wasn't there..." I trailed off, my gaze flicking to the whiteboard. "His car was."

Ben whistled low. "Bingo. And if his phone didn't leave the house, that means Daniel wasn't driving."

Sandra straightened, her brows knitting together. "Then who was?"

I exhaled sharply, my heart thudding as the realization took root. "Who else would have access to his car? His *wife*."

Ben frowned, running a hand through his hair. "Samantha."

The room went still.

"Ben, I need you to check Samantha's phone," I said, tension coiling in my gut. "Does the cell tower data put it at the school Friday evening?"

Ben returned his hand to the monitor, data churning across the screen in an unreadable—to me —jumble.

"You think Samantha Craig killed me?" Sandra asked, her voice barely above a whisper.

I glanced at her. "I don't know, but she's just

made her way to the suspect list." I crossed to the whiteboard and wrote her name in red.

"She had access. The opportunity. But the motive...? That's the part that doesn't make sense. She didn't know about the money; she wasn't wrapped up in Daniel's affairs—at least, not the shady ones. And as far as we know, she and you had no bad blood."

Sandra pressed a hand to her temple, frustration flickering across her ghostly features. "I don't—none of this makes sense."

I turned to her. "You said before that you were supposed to meet someone that night. Could it have been Samantha?"

Sandra's eyes widened. A flicker of something there—recognition? Uncertainty? But then it was gone, lost in the fog of her fractured memory. "I don't know. I had no reason to meet with her."

"Think," I pressed. "Was there anything off? Any interactions you had with her? Anything about Ethan?"

Sandra hesitated. "Only parent-teacher stuff. And that was always with Daniel."

"No history. No bad blood," I repeated, watching her closely.

Sandra shook her head. "Nothing. Samantha had

no reason to hurt me. We barely interacted outside of the usual school-parent meetings. If she came to the school that night, it wasn't because of me."

I sat back, chewing my lip. Samantha had no obvious motive to kill Sandra. As far as I knew, she wasn't tangled up in school politics or Daniel's donation. But that didn't mean she wasn't involved. So, what the hell was she doing there?

The doorbell rang.

I shot Ben and Sandra a look before heading for the door. "Keep searching that data," I told Ben. "Let me know the minute you can confirm she was there."

Bandit, always excited at the chime of the doorbell, beat me to the front door, bouncing up and down. "Mom! Mom! Mom! We have a visitor! Is it Dad?"

I ruffled her ears. "No, sweetheart. Dad wouldn't ring the doorbell."

"That's right," she agreed, head bobbing. "Because this is his home now."

"It is." With a tender smile lingering on my lips, I swung open the door.

Samantha Craig stood on my doorstep, all pleasant smiles and practiced politeness. "Hi, Audrey. Sorry for dropping in like this. I was wondering if I could get my scarf back? The one I lent you the other day?"

I stared at her, every nerve in my body firing at once.

Oh, hell.

There was no proof—*yet*—that she was involved in anything more than poor taste in men. Turning her away would be rude.

I forced a polite smile. "Sure, come in. It's upstairs."

Stepping aside, I let her in. Her gaze flicked around my home, cataloging details like she was taking inventory. Bandit, usually the first to greet guests with her grabby little raccoon hands, lingered in the hallway, ears pinned back. When Samantha crouched as if to pat her, Bandit bolted, scurrying toward the living room, peeking around the corner warily.

I gestured toward the back of the house. "You can wait in the living room. I'll grab it."

Samantha hesitated, then nodded, making her way down the hall as I turned toward the stairs.

Ben, watching intently, muttered, "You *sure* about this, Fitz?"

"Get any hits on that data yet?" I muttered back.

Upstairs, I snatched the scarf off my dresser, my

thoughts racing. Was Samantha really here for it? Or was this just an excuse? When I came back down, Samantha was standing near the kitchen counter, fingers trailing along the edge like she was checking for dust. I resisted the urge to snatch a dishcloth and wipe it down—or tell her to write her name in it if she found any.

Instead, I held up the scarf. "Here you go."

She took it, running the silky fabric through her fingers. "Thanks. Lovely home you have."

I smiled. Or at least, I tried. My face felt tight, the expression teetering dangerously close to a grimace. "Appreciate it."

She tilted her head. "How's the investigation going?"

I shrugged lightly. "Oh, you know. Making progress." Nodding toward the coffee machine, I said, "I was about to make some. Want one?"

She hesitated, like the invitation caught her off guard. "Sure."

I turned my back for *two seconds*. That was all it took.

A sharp pull yanked me backward, the scarf wrapping around my throat in an iron grip. I choked, fingers scrambling against the fabric as Samantha tightened her hold. "You should've left this alone," she hissed into my ear.

A thousand thoughts shot through my brain at once, but the loudest was: *Oh, hell no.*

Ben and Sandra immediately went ballistic.

"AUDREY!" Sandra shrieked.

Ben was practically vibrating with rage. "I *told* you! I TOLD YOU!"

My vision blurred as Samantha hauled back, her grip unrelenting. My fingers clawed at the scarf, trying to pry it loose, but she had leverage, and I was already getting lightheaded.

Fine. Time to get dirty.

I twisted just enough to ram my elbow into her ribs. Hard.

Samantha grunted but didn't let go. Dammit.

All right. *New plan.*

I drove my heel down onto her foot. She yelped, her grip faltering just enough—I spun to face her, snapped my head back, then rocketed forward, colliding with her face in a solid, skull-rattling headbutt.

Pain *exploded* across my forehead.

Samantha shrieked, stumbling back, blood streaming through her fingers.

I groaned, pressing a hand to my forehead. "Oh my God, that was a mistake."

Ben winced. "Yeah, headbutts are, like, fifty percent effective and a hundred percent regrettable."

Samantha, blinking dazedly, snarled and lunged again.

"TASER! BAG! NOW!" Ben yelled, pointing toward my bag on the counter.

I flung myself forward, the momentum sending both of us stumbling. My hand shot out, snagging the strap of my bag. It slid onto the floor, contents spilling everywhere. I scrambled, fingers closing around what I *thought* was my taser. I spun and jabbed it at her, hitting the button.

Nothing happened.

Samantha blinked.

I looked down.

It was a flashlight.

"Oh, for fu—"

Samantha lunged.

I barely managed to grab my bag, dragging it with me as I scrambled backward. Samantha snatched at my ankle, yanking me toward her. I kicked wildly, sending my keys flying across the room. Bandit screamed from under the couch.

Thor perched on the arm of the sofa, his tail

lashing, ears flat against his head. "Do I need to call someone again, or are you planning to get this under control yourself?"

Frantic, I dug into my bag as she clawed at me, fingers scrambling for *anything* that could save my ass. Finally—contact.

I twisted and slammed the taser into her ribs, jamming my thumb onto the button.

A crackling ZZZZT filled the air.

Samantha went rigid, arms flailing like one of those inflatable tube men at a car dealership. She hit the floor in a convulsing heap, eyes wide with shock. A strangled grunt escaped her lips.

And then—oh my god—a fart.

Ben *lost it.*

Sandra clapped a hand over her mouth, eyes round as saucers. "Did she just—"

Ben doubled over, howling. "OH MY GOD, SHE TOTALLY DID!"

Samantha twitched violently, drooling slightly, the smell of burned polyester filling the air.

I sucked in a deep breath, shaking as I fumbled for my phone. When Kade picked up, I rasped, "Hey, babe. You might wanna come home. I, uh... just tased Samantha Craig in the kitchen."

A long pause. Then a sharp inhale. "Do you want to tell me why you tased Samantha Craig?"

"It's not my fault!" I protested. "She tried to *strangle* me!"

That got him moving. "Are you hurt?" His voice sharpened, all business now.

I rubbed my throat, wincing. "I mean, I'll live. *She* might need a minute, though."

Another pause. "Who needs the ambulance more?"

I glanced down at Samantha, still twitching on the floor. "Hard to say."

"Jesus, Audrey. I'm on my way."

I hung up and exhaled, finally taking in the utter disaster zone that was my kitchen. My bag was overturned, my keys were somewhere under the couch, and Samantha Craig was still a drooling, twitching mess at my feet.

Ben grinned. "You gonna sit on her till Kade gets here?"

I considered it. Then, with a sigh, I lowered myself to straddle Samantha and keep her pinned to the floor. *Just in case.* "Guess so."

Sandra, still looking equal parts horrified and impressed, hovered nearby. "So, uh... is she gonna be okay?"

I patted Samantha's shoulder reassuringly. "Yeah, she'll be fine. Feeling should come back to her limbs, eventually."

Samantha let out a pained groan.

I leaned in, dropping my voice conspiratorially. "And, uh... if you *did* pee yourself, totally normal. Happens to the best of us."

Ben *howled*.

Thor stretched, flicking his tail. "After all that excitement, I assume you'll be needing a snack. You know, to keep your sugar levels up. I know I sure do."

And that was how Kade found me when he arrived—sitting on a semi-conscious Samantha Craig, explaining the side effects of a taser while my cat negotiated for snacks.

He stopped in the doorway, took in the scene, and *sighed*.

"Of course," he muttered. "Of course, this is what I walk into."

I shrugged. "Welcome home, honey."

CHAPTER TWENTY-THREE

Kade's gaze snapped to me. "Audrey."

I swallowed. "Yes, dear?"

"What. The hell. Happened?"

"Well," I said. "Samantha tried to strangle me, so I tased her. Then she farted." I gestured vaguely toward the woman under me. "And now she's drooling. And has possibly peed herself. Jury's still out on that one."

Kade blinked. "She farted?"

"Loudly," I confirmed with a nod. Ben snickered and added, unhelpfully, "Almost poetic, really."

Kade pinched the bridge of his nose like he was developing a migraine. "And why did she try to strangle you?"

I looked down at Samantha, whose face was currently pressed against my kitchen tiles. "I dunno. Maybe ask her?"

Samantha groaned, finally regaining some motor function. "Get off me, you crazy—"

I squeezed my knees a little harder into her sides. "I'd watch how you finish that sentence."

Kade kneeled down, cuffing her wrists. "Samantha Craig, you're under arrest for assault and attempted murder, and I have a feeling we're gonna be adding a whole lot more to that charge."

Samantha hissed. "I didn't kill anyone."

I snorted. "You sure about that?" I shuffled to the side, sitting on the floor, rubbing my throat. "Because I've been putting this puzzle together, and all signs point to you."

She glared at me, but there was a flicker of uncertainty in her eyes.

I folded my arms. "You told Sandra you had a meeting with her that night. But that was a lie, wasn't it?"

Samantha's jaw clenched.

I pressed on. "You needed a way inside the school. So, you caught Sandra off guard, made her second-guess herself. Made it seem like she was the one who forgot. And because she was the kind of person who took her job seriously, she let you in."

Sandra, frozen by the dining room table, sucked in a sharp breath. I kept going. "But there was no meeting. You weren't there to talk. You were there to confront her."

Samantha's expression darkened, but she still refused to speak.

"You knew Daniel was up to something—maybe even suspected another affair—but you couldn't just follow him. You were stuck at home with the kids. So you waited until he got back, then took his car instead of your own. Not something you usually do, but you wanted access to his GPS history—to see exactly where he'd been."

Samantha's nostrils flared.

"And where did that lead you? The school. And who did you find? Sandra."

Silence.

"You assumed the worst. That she was another one of his affairs, another woman he was sneaking around with. And instead of thinking logically— like, I don't know, maybe *asking* a single damn question—you lost your mind."

Her nostrils flared. "She was ruining my family."

I barked out a laugh. "No, sweetheart. Your

husband ruined your family. Sandra was literally at work, grading papers. But you were so blinded by jealousy you killed an innocent woman over nothing."

Samantha's breathing turned erratic, the realization sinking in.

Behind me, Sandra let out a shaky breath. "She lied to me."

My chest tightened, but I didn't turn. "And then you tried to kill me because you knew I'd figure it out. Which, by the way, is incredibly insulting because *obviously* I was going to figure it out."

Ben leaned against the counter, shaking his head. "People never learn."

Kade stood, pulling her to her feet. "Let's go." She groaned, her head lolling to the side, still too out of it to put up much of a fight as he led her out the door.

The second they were gone, a hush settled over the room. Sandra exhaled softly. "So... this is it."

"Looks like," I agreed.

She looked down at her hands, flexing her fingers as if testing her own existence. "I didn't think this moment would come so soon."

"You deserve peace, Sandra," I said gently. "It's time."

Her eyes glistened, and she gave a watery smile. "Yeah. I guess it is."

A soft glow surrounded her, the familiar pull of whatever lay beyond calling her forward. She took a shaky breath and met my gaze. "Thank you, Audrey. For everything."

I forced a smile, my throat tight. "Go on. Before I start crying and ruin my reputation."

She chuckled, then turned to Ben. "Guess you're stuck here, huh?"

Ben smirked. "Yeah, well. Somebody's gotta keep an eye on Fitz."

Sandra rolled her eyes. "Poor you." Then, with one last nod, she stepped toward the light. It enveloped her, warm and golden, and just like that —she was gone.

The room felt emptier. Lighter.

I exhaled slowly, pressing my lips together as I blinked up at the ceiling. *Not crying. Not crying.*

A moment later, Kade stepped back inside, his sharp gaze immediately locking onto me. "Jesus, Audrey, your throat—"

I waved him off. "It's fine. I've had worse."

His expression darkened. "That's not reassuring."

I gave him my best smile. "All I need is coffee."

Kade raked a hand through his hair, exhaling heavily. "Fine. You sit. I'll make the coffee."

I moved to the couch, letting my head fall back. My limbs felt like jelly, my forehead throbbed, but at least I was still breathing. Bandit jumped onto my lap, patting my arm like she was checking for injuries. "Mom is still alive!" she announced to no one in particular.

"Barely," Thor grumbled from the armrest. "I'd ask if she brought snacks, but she looks half dead."

"That's just her default setting," Ben teased, but I didn't miss the underlying concern in his voice. He was used to me getting into scrapes, but this one had been a little too close for comfort.

Kade busied himself in the kitchen, filling the coffeepot with water. "So, here's where things stand," he called over his shoulder. "Claire is out. Her resignation will hit the board in the morning. Whether she faces charges will depend on how deep this fraud investigation goes. Priscilla, as much as I'd love to arrest her on principle, isn't facing anything. Daniel and Lyle, though? That's a mess. Both pointing fingers, both in cuffs, and both up to their necks in financial crimes."

I let out a low whistle. "So, they'll both go down?"

"Probably. Might take a while to untangle, but neither of them is walking away clean."

He poured two cups of coffee and had taken a step toward me when my gaze landed on the smear on my shirt.

"Oh, come on." I peeled the shirt away from my chest. "Is that blood?"

"Not yours," Kade assured me.

"Great. Wonderful. Perfect." I flung my arm out, gesturing to my entire outfit. "This was a perfectly good shirt! And my jeans!" I stretched a leg out, jostling Bandit in the process. "Do you know how hard it is to find jeans that actually fit my butt without cutting off circulation?"

Kade looked like he was trying not to laugh. "To be fair, you did headbutt her."

"One day, I'm gonna get through a case without staining something, and it's gonna feel so unnatural I'll probably panic." Bandit patted my arm, as if to say 'it's okay', while Thor turned to look at the wall.

Kade handed me a coffee then sat down beside me, pulling me close. I took a fortifying sip, noticing the smear of blood on my wrist as I lowered my cup. "Perfect. More blood."

With a sigh, I flopped back against the cushion, eyes closed. "At least my streak's intact."

"What streak?"

I cracked open an eye. "It's not a real day until I spill something on myself."

He chuckled, dropping a kiss on the top of my head.

We sat in companionable silence for a few minutes, allowing the coffee to work its magic and revive my soul.

"What do you think will happen to Samantha?" I asked, voice muffled against his chest.

"She's got nothing left to lose, so I expect we'll have some answers soon." Kade took a sip of his coffee, then chuckled. "Oh, and you're gonna love this—turns out the guy who jumped into the water? Not our guy."

"No?"

"Patrol pulled him over for speeding. Sergeant Powell walks up, notices the guy's soaking wet, and before they even ask a question, he just starts panicking and spills everything."

"Which is?"

"That he saw us down at the dock, recognized I was a cop, and freaked out, thinking I was there to arrest him for unpaid fines. So, he jumped into the ocean to get away."

I lifted my head. "Wait, wait, wait. He jumped into the ocean over unpaid fines?"

Kade shrugged. "Apparently, he thought there was a warrant out for his arrest."

I blinked. "Was there?"

"Nope."

I let that sink in for a moment, then shifted slightly, my brain still piecing together the last few threads. "And that burner phone message—'usual place. 8PM.' That wasn't about Sandra, was it?"

Kade shook his head. "Nope. We checked the phone records. That was Daniel and Claire arranging one of their motel meetups. Nothing to do with the murder."

I huffed out a breath. "All that drama for a sleazy affair. Classy."

Shaking my head, I let my eyes drift shut, sinking back against Kade's warmth.

"Before you conk out completely," Ben said from the armchair opposite, "I got the data you wanted. It's confirmed—Samantha's phone pinged off the cell tower, putting her at the school Friday night."

I cracked one eye open. "Yeah?"

Kade glanced down. "What's that?"

I waved a lazy hand. "Ben said to double check the

cell tower data. Samantha's phone pinged at the school that night. Get your tech guys to comb through it, and you'll have the proof you need to place her at the scene."

"That's what I needed," Kade muttered, already pulling out his phone. "Thanks, Ben," he said to where he *thought* Ben was sitting. Which, of course, he wasn't.

I half-smiled, sipping my coffee, exhaustion creeping over me. My eyelids drooped. Kade's heartbeat was steady against my ear, and Bandit curled up tighter in my lap. Thor shifted just enough to press against my side. A grudging show of solidarity.

I drifted off.

A voice pulled me from sleep sometime later. Deep, low, and familiar.

Kade.

"Yeah," he murmured, phone pressed to his ear. "Good job, guys. We've got her."

I cracked an eye open. The room was dimmer now, the coffee table lamp casting a warm glow. Ben glanced at the clock on the wall. "Huh. Is that the time? Stephen York usually watches *Matlock* right about now." And just like that, he vanished.

I yawned and stretched, blinking up at Kade. He

glanced down at me, lips quirking. "How you feeling?"

I thought about it. "Like I got strangled and then electrocuted someone. So, you know. Average day."

He huffed out a laugh and brushed his fingers through my hair, careful to avoid the lump on my forehead. "That was the station. Samantha's lawyer has arrived. I'm betting it won't be long before she folds."

I sighed, sinking back into his warmth and letting my eyes drift shut again. "Perfect. So sad, though, that Samantha was trying to figure out where he'd been and who he'd been seeing, and when she got to the school, she just... assumed. She found Sandra there—alone— and convinced herself she was the one fooling around with her husband. Poor Sandra. That's so unfair."

"Life's unfair sometimes, babe," Kade agreed.

Bandit let out a sleepy chitter from my lap, curling tighter against me. Thor, sprawled along my side, released a dramatic sigh of his own, no doubt dreaming of unlimited kibble. The house was quiet, warm, safe.

Until it wasn't.

A chill prickled across my skin. The shift in the air yanked me from the edge of sleep. My eyes snapped open. A figure moved through the living room. My first thought was Ben, but no—Ben had presence, a way of making himself known even when he wasn't talking. This? This was different.

The figure never stopped. Never looked at me. Never spoke. It walked straight through the wall. My breath stalled. My heart slammed against my ribs.

Kade stirred beside me. "Audrey?" His voice was thick with concern.

I barely heard him. My eyes were locked on the empty space where the ghost had passed through.

Seb.

And dangling from his fingers? A plush rabbit.

THE END

Gasping at that ending? I know — I'm the worst. But if you want a little something to tide you over until the next book, sign up for my newsletter and get an exclusive bonus scene told from Kade's point of view.

It's all yours at:

https://janehinchey.com/ghost-and-tell-bonus-scene.

#5 Witch Way to Death & Destruction

#6 Witch Way to Secrets & Sorcery

The Gravestone Mysteries

#1 Fur the Hex of it

#2 Battle of the Hexes

#3 What the Hex

The Midnight Chronicles

#1 One Minute to Midnight

#2 Two Minutes Past Midnight

#3 Third Strike of Midnight

Clean Scene Inc.

#1 All in Vein

PARANORMAL ROMANCE/URBAN FANTASY

The Awakening Trilogy

Hell's Angel Trilogy

The Enforcer Series (4 books)

Standalones

Returned

Secret Fates

ABOUT JANE

Jane Hinchey writes fast-paced, snark-filled cozy mysteries packed with quirky characters, small-town scandals, and mischievous animals who tend to steal the spotlight (and the snacks). Her books blend humor, heart, and a dash of romance — perfect for readers who love a twisty mystery served with a side of sass.

When Jane's not plotting fictional murders, you'll find her wrangling her two real-life feline overlords, Maxx and Morgan, or refereeing her backyard turtle, Squirt — the self-proclaimed pond cat.

Born in the UK, raised in Australia, and now living in Adelaide, Jane spends her days writing, reading, and hunting for the perfect donut.

For bonus scenes, sneak peeks, and behind-the-scenes chaos, visit www.janehinchey.com.

facebook.com/janehincheyauthor

instagram.com/janehincheyauthor

amazon.com/Jane-Hinchey/e/B0I93449MI

bookbub.com/authors/jane-hinchey

goodreads.com/jane_hinchey